HOW TO SAVE A LIFE

How To Save A Life

…Marli felt the stranger's eyes on her again. She doggedly avoided looking at him, instead continuing her scan of the bar.

"You like country music?"

She repressed a sigh. Had this happened a few weeks ago, making small talk with a handsome man would have been a given. The way *he* looked—a *definite* given. But not now.

"I hate country music."

"Ah. So…what's a gorgeous girl like you doing here…all alone in a country bar…drinking Diet Coke?"

"There's an original line." She tried to give him a freezing look. She wasn't very good at it. On the contrary—apparently something about her attracted men like wasps to syrup, without her even trying. Which had led to the whole big freaking mess her life was in.

"It wasn't a line," he muttered. "I'm not trying to pick you up. Just making conversation."

She pressed her lips together and looked away, then back, studying him out of the corner of her eye. Talk about tall, dark and handsome. But not handsome in a pretty-boy way. His face was tough looking, square-jawed, serious, his mouth firm and straight. But when he'd smiled…whew. It was enough to make a girl's panties damp and her nipples hard.

And he was big. He took up all his own space and some of hers. His faded jeans covered thick, muscular thighs. His white button-up shirt didn't hide the flat muscles of his chest and the bulge of biceps beneath the thin cotton. Big hands held his beer bottle, which he'd been drinking very slowly, the turned-back cuffs of his shirt revealing strong wrists. He gave off an aura of safety. Protection. Awareness tingled; attraction sparked inside her. *Damn. Talk about crappy timing…*

Also By Kelly Jamieson

Worth Waiting For

HOW TO SAVE A LIFE

BY

KELLY JAMIESON

AMBER QUILL PRESS, LLC
http://www.amberquill.com

HOW TO SAVE A LIFE
AN AMBER QUILL PRESS BOOK

Amber Quill Press, LLC
http://www.amberquill.com

ISBN 978-1-60272-850-9

Layout and Formatting provided by: ElementalAlchemy.com

PUBLISHED IN THE UNITED STATES OF AMERICA

CHAPTER 1

She was looking for a man.

Marli couldn't sit at home submerged in grief and guilt any longer. Returning to the location of her ultimate shame made her skin crawl and her stomach tighten unpleasantly, but she didn't know how else to get out of the sinkhole her life had become, how else to dig herself out of this crater of depression and blame.

She surveyed Cactus Jack's Saloon, scanning the face of every man leaning against a rough wooden post chatting up a woman, every guy sitting at the long bar nursing a beer, every male partner two-stepping on the dance floor to the twang of steel guitars.

Marli swept her gaze across the crowded tables. From her seat at the end of the bar, she had a view of the entire saloon. *Perfect.*

She sipped her Diet Coke. She liked sleek, sexy clubs with throbbing techno dance music and people dressed in trendy clothes, not blue jeans and cowboy boots. But Cactus Jack's had been Krista's favorite place.

Memories of the last night she'd been there played through Marli's head like a movie trailer. Krista laughing and dancing with that guy…Ron. The way Ron had looked Marli up and down. Krista accusing her of flirting with Ron. Krista leaving with Ron, and the way he'd turned and smirked at Marli as they'd walked out.

Marli shuddered.

Someone slid onto the barstool next to her, and Marli's stomach jolted with nerves. Her gaze flew to his face, expecting dark eyes and a blond moustache. But she met flame-blue eyes in a clean-shaven face. Strong. Square jaw, nice mouth. Gorgeous.

She drew in a shaky breath and turned away from the handsome stranger, relief and adrenaline sliding through her body.

"Sorry," he murmured. "Didn't mean to startle you. Is this seat taken?"

"No." She didn't look at him. He wasn't what she was looking for. She tightened her grip on the icy-slick glass of cola and directed her gaze back out to the rowdy bar.

"Are you meeting someone here?" the man asked. "If he shows up, just let me know and I'll move."

"I'm not meeting anyone," she said quietly. "I'm kind of looking for someone, but he's not here."

"Well, if you see him, just let me know."

Yeah, right. "Sure."

The bartender appeared in front of them. "Surf Coast Pale Ale," the stranger requested. "Can I order food here?"

"You bet." The bartender slapped a laminated menu onto the bar, looked at Marli. "Another Diet Coke?"

She nodded, swirled the melting ice in her glass and finished it off.

"I'll have a steak—medium rare. And fries." The man handed the menu over to the bartender, who disappeared with it.

Marli felt the stranger's eyes on her again. She doggedly avoided looking at him, instead continuing her scan of the bar.

"You like country music?"

She repressed a sigh. Had this happened a few weeks ago, making small talk with a handsome man would have been a given. The way *he* looked—a *definite* given. But not now.

"I hate country music."

"Ah. So…what's a gorgeous girl like you doing here…all alone in a country bar…drinking Diet Coke?"

"There's an original line." She tried to give him a freezing look. She wasn't very good at it. On the contrary—apparently something about her attracted men like wasps to syrup, without her even trying. Which had led to the whole big freaking mess her life was in.

"It wasn't a line," he muttered. "I'm not trying to pick you up. Just making conversation."

She pressed her lips together and looked away, then back, studying him out of the corner of her eye. Talk about tall, dark and handsome. But not handsome in a pretty-boy way. His face was tough looking, square-jawed, serious, his mouth firm and straight. But when he'd smiled…whew. It was enough to make a girl's panties damp and her nipples hard.

And he was big. He took up all his own space and some of hers. His faded jeans covered thick, muscular thighs. His white button-up shirt didn't hide the flat muscles of his chest and the bulge of biceps beneath the thin cotton. Big hands held his beer bottle, which he'd been drinking very slowly, the turned-back cuffs of his shirt revealing strong wrists. He gave off an aura of safety. Protection. Awareness tingled; attraction sparked inside her. *Damn. Talk about crappy timing.*

"We could talk about something else," he said finally. "How about sports?"

"Go, Dodgers."

"No! You gotta be a Padres fan."

She had to ask. "You're from San Diego?"

"Yeah."

"So what are you doing here in Rocky Harbor?"

His mouth twisted. "I'm on a leave from my job. I'm on my way up to San Francisco to visit a buddy of mine. Got this far and stopped here for a while."

"Oh. What do you do for a living?"

He didn't answer for a long moment, and Marli cursed herself for asking. Why was she even talking to this guy? Was she nuts? After what happened to Krista, she was *crazy* to be sitting here talking to a stranger like this.

"I'm an FBI agent."

Oh. Well. "Really," she said slowly. Her tense body relaxed minutely. With his size, his rough good looks, the intensity of his gaze, he should have made her feel intimidated, but he didn't. Other than the dangerous sexuality that was most definitely threatening. *An FBI agent. Huh.*

He shrugged, turned the beer bottle in his hands. "How about you? What do you do?"

"I'm a photographer."

"What do you photograph?"

"Commercial stuff. Advertising, some magazine work."

He made an impressed faced. "You have your own business?"

"Yes. But right now it just seems so…unimportant."

"Yeah. When crap happens, everything else seems trivial."

"You sound like you've been there."

"Yeah. Been there. Done that. Screwed up big time."

"Want to talk about it?"

His mouth twisted wryly. "Not really."

"Okay. I get it."

Their eyes met and they stared at each other for a long moment. Attraction tugged at her, a connection drew her to him, and something softened and expanded in her chest. She blinked and looked away.

The bartender appeared with the stranger's steak dinner.

The smell of the charbroiled meat and golden, greasy fries wafted toward Marli and made her mouth water. Funny. She hadn't had any appetite lately.

She turned away from him to let him eat. "Have some fries," he offered, motioning to the huge mound of them on the plate.

"No, thanks."

He cut into the steak, and they sat in silence while he ate his dinner, the twang and dip of country music growing louder as the night wore on.

Out of the corner of her eye, she saw him lay his knife and fork on the empty plate. "I can't believe you ate the whole thing," she remarked. It had been a generous steak.

He grinned. "Trying to bulk up."

She looked him up and down. "You don't need to bulk up. You look great." She closed her eyes. *Shit!* She was *not* flirting. It had just popped out of her mouth…and…and it was only the truth!

"Uh…thanks." He crumpled up the paper napkin and tossed it onto the plate, pushed it away from him. He took a swallow of his beer. "So…wanna dance?"

"No, no thanks."

"Come on."

His sexy voice tempted Marli. She loved dancing. She loved men. She loved—correction—she *used to* love having fun. She wasn't here for fun tonight.

"I said no thanks."

"Hey, no problem." He put his hands in the air.

He turned his head and lifted a hand to catch the attention of the bartender, who was down at the other end mixing some drinks.

"Can I buy you another drink?" he offered. "Hey, I'm Trey, by the way."

"Nice to meet you, Trey," she said, sliding off the stool. "I'm leaving."

* * *

"Wait!" Trey put a hand on the pretty blonde's arm.

Panic flashed in her amazing green-gold eyes. This was one jumpy woman.

"Wait," he said again, softly. "Don't go on my account. I'll leave you alone, if that's what you want."

She stopped, looked down at his hand on her arm and jerked away from him.

"Really. I'm not trying to pick you up or anything. I wouldn't even know how." He grimaced self-deprecatingly. "I'm sorry if I was bothering you."

He didn't care if she stayed or left. Except—she did intrigue him.

Light reddish-gold hair hung down her back in long spirals, hair that he wanted to fill his hands with. She had the biggest, most expressive green eyes he'd ever seen, and the overwhelming sadness in them made his breath stick in his chest.

"I don't need another drink." She sat down again.

She wasn't leaving. *Whew.* The relief shifting through him was crazy, since he'd just told her he'd leave her alone. "Are you sure? I'd even spring for a beer, if you wanted one."

She smiled crookedly.

"Seriously," he said, "if you want me to stop talking to you, just say so. I'll go sit somewhere else." He met her eyes. What had put that nervous shimmer in them?

"You don't have to move. Just know that I don't pick up strange guys in bars. I don't let them buy me drinks, I don't dance with them, and I *don't* flirt with them."

"Hey." Her vehement protests made him wonder what had happened to her. He put a hand on his chest as if wounded. "I'm not strange."

She choked out a laugh, and for some reason it made him feel…proud. Like he'd done something good for a change. "I mean, I don't *know* you."

He studied her out of the corner of his eye. She was slim, but full breasts pushed against a thin white T-shirt. She sat with one long, long leg crossed over the other, wearing jeans and a pair of pointy-toed shoes, one of which hung from the toe of the top foot in a sexy, inviting way. He couldn't take his eyes off that foot, gently swinging in time to the music. Even though she hated country music. Her green eyes had little flecks of gold that made them sparkle. There was a lot of life in those eyes, even though her face was serious.

Now what? It had been a hell of a long time since he'd tried to make conversation with a girl in a bar. Not that he was trying to pick her up. He was just curious.

"You look like you need cheering up," he commented, changing the subject and taking another swig of his Pale Ale.

One corner of her mouth turned up. "I don't think that's possible."

"Wow. Sounds pretty bad."

"My life is shit right now," she said. "You don't even want to *try* to cheer me up. You should go find someone else if you want to have some fun."

He looked back at her steadily. "I'm not looking for fun," he said. "My life is shit right now, too. Maybe we could just keep each company in our misery."

He had her attention again. Her lips curved into a reluctant smile. "We're pretty pathetic, aren't we?"

He grinned. Saw her eyes widen in response. Liked it. His body responded with a tightening in his groin. "Yeah."

"Listen, would you at least tell me your name?"

She pursed those pretty lips, and his cock twitched. "It's Marli."

"Marli," he repeated. "I like it."

"I really shouldn't be doing this."

"Doing what?"

"Talking to you." She bit her lower lip in a sexy nibble. "Look, you seem really nice and...well, really hot." She closed her eyes, putting a hand to her forehead. "Damn."

He stared at her, arousal comingling with bemusement.

"I like talking to you," she continued, "but I can't do this. I can't be...having fun."

He knew only too well what she meant. "Yeah, I know. You're not allowed to have fun or enjoy yourself. The world should just stop and know your pain. Isn't that right?"

She drew in a long breath. "Yes."

"It seems weird that normal life goes on, doesn't it?" He lifted a hand to all the people around them, laughing, dancing, oblivious.

"Will it...get better? Will that feeling ever go away?"

"I'll let you know if it does." He paused. "I'm kidding. It's a cliché, but life does go on, Marli. I've been wallowing too long. You aren't the only one who's been enjoying yourself tonight."

He didn't want to scare her away. Christ, she was jumpy as a grasshopper. But he had to admit he was interested and attracted.

"This is the first time in a long time I've felt…well, felt anything," he continued. "Felt hungry. Felt amused. Felt…turned on." He met her eyes steadily.

"I really have to go." She grabbed her purse and stood up. Then she stopped. "'Bye, Trey. It was nice to meet you."

Damn. He'd said too much. Disappointment settled over him, slow and heavy, but this time he didn't try to stop her as she threaded her way through the crowded bar and out the door.

CHAPTER 2

Sheldon lay on the bed in his dingy motel room, arms behind his head. When he'd left the bar that night, he'd turned around and looked at Marli—*that bitch*—and he'd seen her eyes widen in response. She'd had no idea what he'd been about to do.

Oh, man, that had been sweet. Krista had been so utterly terrified when he'd pulled out the knife. She'd tried to run, but he was too fast. He'd grabbed her… He replayed the video in his mind, almost enjoying it more the second time around.

He put a hand to the hard-on behind his fly and rubbed. His cock twitched and thickened, his balls drew up and his skin tingled. He was getting excited all over again. The power. There was no greater power than completely dominating someone, inflicting pain. And she'd deserved it. She was a woman, not as much of a slut as her friend Marli, but all women were whores.

He couldn't stop thinking about Marli, that tall, blonde bitch. Krista's friend. What a slut she was, flirting with all those men. But when *he* wanted to flirt with her, she'd cut him dead. *Ha. Dead.* A laugh gurgled inside him. That was funny, considering what happened to her friend.

Marli'd flirted with him, then rejected him. She'd *laughed* at him, laughed at him being a cowboy. Heat built in his chest and in his head at the memory.

His mother's face flashed through his mind, her laughing mouth and mocking eyes.

That wasn't how it worked. When he wanted a woman, he got her. Then he could do what he wanted with her. Like all the others.

They all deserved what they got. Krista had changed her mind about going with him the moment they'd gotten in his car. She'd tried to get away, and he'd had to stop her. It hadn't gone the way he'd planned it. He glanced over at the closet in his motel room. *Ah, well.*

He sat up and punched the crappy cheap pillows, then stuffed them back behind him. He gave some thought to his plans. He didn't want to wait around too long because they were looking for him. He knew it. He saw the news on TV. Usually, he left town right away, but this time Marli's taunting smile had kept his anger simmering. Marli was going to pay for laughing at him. Just like his mother.

It was dangerous, staying here. He never stuck around after he was done with a woman. His blood sizzled through his veins.

If he was going to stay in Rocky Harbor, he had to change his appearance. He hadn't had much cash. The fifty bucks he'd taken out of Krista's purse he'd used for a trip to Long Drugs for some hair dye and a pair of scissors. But the money hadn't lasted long and now he'd been hit with a genius idea.

He could kill two birds with one stone—get a job and keep an eye out for Marli.

He grinned up at the ceiling.

* * *

Marli emerged from Cactus Jack's onto the dark sidewalk and glanced around. There were a few people on the street, but her stomach quivered and her muscles tightened. Guilt, anger and lack of sleep had shredded her nerves over the past two weeks, eating away at them until she was on edge all the time. She hurried to her car, parked in a nearby parking garage. Damn, she hated parking garages.

Sounds bounced off the concrete floors and walls, and twice she stopped to listen, heart in her throat, convinced she'd heard another set of footsteps behind her. But it was just the echo of her own shoes on the cement.

She locked the doors as soon as she got into the car, having quickly assessed the back seat to make sure it was empty. She sat there for a moment, gripping the steering wheel, taking deep breaths and trying to slow her racing heart.

Usually a young kid worked in this parking garage, but tonight she was glad it was a man around her age. It made her feel minutely safer as she handed over her money and waited for the arm to rise so she could exit.

Tonight her anxiety levels were escalated by the sexual tension that had simmered between Trey and her for the last two hours. She hadn't been running; there'd been nothing to make her heart beat more quickly, no trigger for her rapid breathing in the bar. It was *him*. He'd gotten her all agitated, even more than she already was. That was the *last* thing she needed right now.

He made her curious. He was interesting. Dangerous, yet protective. A cop, a big jock football player, but with intelligence and hints of pain in those intense blue eyes. He made her feel warm and shivery, and damn it, watching those long, sexy fingers of his made her think about having those hands on her body.

He was a stranger passing through town, and she'd never see him again. Instead of calming her, the thought was strangely disappointing.

She drove home and parked in the driveway in front of her duplex condo, lit up like an office tower in downtown LA. She'd left all the lights on, to hell with the electricity bill she was going to get. For the last few weeks, she'd even slept with the lights on.

She slipped in through her front door and locked it behind her. Usually she took such pleasure in walking into her small home. She'd finally made enough money to buy her own place and she loved it. Sleek and modern, it was just her style, with open rooms, pale maple floors and chrome accents. But tonight she didn't feel pleasure because it looked nice. Tonight, she just felt relief at locking the door behind her and closing out the world.

Taking a deep breath now she was in the sanctuary of her home, she dropped her purse on the side table and went up the stairs to her bedroom, leaving the lights blazing. In her bedroom, she kicked off her shoes and shimmied out of her jeans. In her T-shirt and panties, she walked into the adjoining bathroom. Slate tiles in warm shades of grey and taupe covered the floor and walls. The huge spa tub occupied most of the space, with a separate shower enclosed in glass walls. Her own private retreat.

She was so wound up she knew she'd never sleep. She'd only been sleeping a couple of hours a night for the last few weeks, and when she did sleep, nightmares jolted her awake. A bath would help relax her. Soon steam filled the room and she slipped into the blissful, warm embrace of the water, the muted rumble of the jets blocking out all other sound.

* * *

It wasn't the fine cuisine or even the Pale Ale that drew Trey back to Cactus Jack's the next night. Rather, it was this strange, irrational belief he might see Marli.

He had no idea why she'd been there, sitting all by herself, checking out everyone in the place, even though she hated country music and didn't drink. She was such a mystery.

He liked a mystery, liked solving puzzles, finding answers.

She made him curious.

Once again he headed to the bar, liking the end seat where Marli had been last night so he could see the entire room.

A different bartender was working tonight. Trey ordered another Surf Coast Pale Ale. While he waited, he surveyed the bar, much as Marli had last night.

No Marli. He glanced at his watch. *Still early.*

He watched people dancing and having fun. It was amazing how alone you could feel in a crowded bar. Even more alone than he felt at night sitting in his empty apartment. He nursed his beer, sweeping the room with his eyes.

For some reason—he had no idea why—he turned his head and there she was, looking right at him from the other side of the L-shaped bar. Her gaze met his at that exact moment. Her eyes widened in surprise.

He just looked at her, waiting. Would she come over? He resisted the urge to beckon her over. If she didn't come, he'd go over there. But not right away.

She was skittish and any hint of pushing on his part made her back off. He didn't want to scare her, so he waited, tapping his fingers on the bar.

She hesitated, then she slowly moved forward.

He smiled, looked down at his hands clasping the beer bottle and waited. When he sensed her next to him, he looked up. "Hi."

"Hi." Her smile was tentative. "Um…anyone sitting here?" She gestured at the stool beside him. He shook his head.

She slid onto the stool.

"Back again to drink soda and listen to bad music?"

Her lips curved in a hesitant smile. "Yeah."

Trey looked for the bartender to order her a drink. The bartender glanced their way, and Trey lifted a hand, but the guy turned away. Trey frowned. *Huh. No tip for him.* But a moment later the bartender arrived to take their order. Trey ordered another beer and glanced at Marli. "Diet Coke?"

"Yes, please."

When the bartender slid a large glass across the bar to her, she sent him a quick smile of thanks.

"So you're still in town," she said. "I thought you'd be on your way to San Francisco."

He shrugged. "It's nice here."

"Yeah. Rocky Harbor's a nice town."

"Maybe tonight you'll dance with me," he suggested softly. "Since now I'm not so strange."

She smiled, but her eyes were guarded. "Maybe," she said. "But you're still a stranger. Really."

"It's funny how I feel I know you, though."

She looked away from him, across the bar. "Yeah, I know."

He watched her breasts rise as she took a deep breath. She wore jeans again, skinny jeans with a long, floaty, green top and round-toed flat shoes.

"Would you like something to eat?" Trey asked.

Her eyes came back to him, green and gold and sparkly. "Are you having another steak?"

"Nah. I ate already. Just wondered if you were hungry."

She considered that. "You know, I *could* eat."

Trey had a feeling he wasn't the only one who'd been skipping meals lately. He grabbed a menu from a stack at the end of the bar and handed her one.

"Would you share some nachos with me?" she asked after a moment of perusing the menu.

"Sure." Again, he got the bartender's attention. The guy sidled up to him, barely looking at him, and Trey ordered the food.

With a grunt, the bartender disappeared. Trey shrugged. "Not very talkative, for a bartender," he commented. "Did you work today?"

"I tried. I've had a hard time focusing lately. But I have contracts, obligations…" She sighed. "My heart's not in it right now, though."

"You know, it helps to talk sometimes."

She eyed him. "Do you follow your own advice, pal?"

"Okay, you got me. Never mind."

"You know, if I was going to talk to anyone, it might be you."

"Why is that?"

"I don't know." She tipped her head to one side. Her long curls swung down past one shoulder. "You give this impression of…security. Like you don't judge people."

"Are you afraid of being judged?"

Her eyes lowered. "Yes."

"Why, Marli?"

She still didn't look up. One finger traced the condensation up and down the big glass she held. She bit her lip. "I'm… I did something awful. In fact, I'm so…angry, disgusted and ashamed of myself. I feel like a monster."

He stiffened. "God, no," he protested. "I hardly know you, but I do know you're not a monster."

"I am. You'd hate me if you knew."

"Why don't you try me?"

"You know," she said slowly, "maybe you *could* help me." Then she shook her head. "Nah, never mind. You're just passing through."

"Help you with what?" His curiosity aroused, he turned his body to face her.

She eyed him. "Never mind."

"Just tell me," he said. "If it's something I can help with, I will."

"It's a long story." She bent her head and her long curls hid her face.

"I got all night."

"Okay." She blew out a long breath, lifted her big, tortured eyes to meet his. "My best friend was murdered."

CHAPTER 3

Oh, Christ. He couldn't speak. Just stared at her.

The bartender slid a plate of nachos onto the bar in front of them. They both ignored it.

"We...we'd been here that night," Marli continued, her voice low but controlled. "At Cactus Jack's. Krista and I, and some other friends of ours. We were celebrating her new job. She met a guy...she really liked him. They left together. The next day, she didn't show up for work. Nobody knew where she was." She swallowed a sob. "The police found her car with her body in it. She'd been raped and s-s-stabbed. And her car was set on f -fire with her in it."

A chill ran down Trey's spine. "Holy Christ."

She nodded and brushed moisture from her eyes. "The guy she left with that night had to have been the one who did it. I thought... I know it's crazy, but I thought maybe he'd come back here. To the bar."

His heart lurched to a stop. "You're not serious. Is that who you're looking for?"

She nodded. "I saw him that night. I got a really good look at him because he was flirting with me a bit, too. I'll know him if I see him."

"What the hell do you think you're going to do if you see him? Jesus, Marli."

"I don't know. Call the police." Then she made a rude noise. "They aren't doing anything about it."

"That's crazy. I'm sure they're investigating it."

"You said you're an FBI agent." She looked up at him. "That's why

I thought maybe you could help somehow."

He made a noise that was almost a growl. "When did this happen?"

"Two weeks ago." She dug into her purse and pulled out her wallet, found a small photograph and handed it to him.

Trey gazed down at the image of a very pretty woman. The candid photograph captured her quiet reserve. His eyes narrowed as he took in her heart-shaped face and long, platinum blonde hair.

"This is Krista," Marli said, her voice thick. "She was my best friend."

"She was blonde," he murmured.

Marli nodded. "Yeah. I was always jealous of her perfect straight hair."

He looked up at her. He loved Marli's hair, the way it bounced and gleamed with fiery highlights. His gut clenched hard. "You're blonde, too."

She blinked at him.

"What do you know about the case? What have the cops told you?" he asked, the hairs on the back of his neck lifting.

"Not much. I heard more on the news than I heard from them. They interviewed me a million times, until I barely remembered my own name. But they sure didn't tell me much."

"They have a suspect?"

"Oh, yeah. It was all over the news." She gulped. "Apparently some serial killer. He's been traveling across the country raping and killing women."

Trey froze. His skin went iceberg cold. *Son of a bitch.*

Time stood still as he processed what was going on here. It was un-fucking-believable. The room shifted out of focus, then back in.

Marli shuddered and swallowed hard. "That bastard. I can't believe… Oh, shit." The tears started again and she furiously wiped them away with her fingers. "Damn it."

"It's okay." He set the photograph carefully on the bar. He brushed her tears away gently with his fingertips. "It's okay."

Why the hell hadn't he heard about this? *Jesus Christ.* Sheldon Barnes had killed again, and where had *he* been? Wallowing in self-pity. He hadn't been watching the news at all lately, and no one from the Bureau had bothered to pick up the phone and tell him. *Shit.* Guilt struck him like hammer blows.

"Not only is it hard because she died, and how she died…but I've been a basket case ever since." She drew in a long breath. "The cops told me not to worry, said if it is this guy, he doesn't usually stick around. He takes off for somewhere else."

"That's true," he murmured.

She opened her mouth, then closed it. "What do you mean, 'that's true'?"

His lips twisted and he ran his tongue over his teeth. He needed to think.

Now he understood the shadows he'd seen in Marli's beautiful eyes. She was nuts, of course, even to think of trying to find Sheldon Barnes, although he couldn't help but admire her courage. After everything she'd been through, it was a wonder she wasn't cowering in her house twenty-four-seven. He didn't know whether to be impressed or pissed. This was one gutsy woman.

But, overwhelming guilt poured through him. That motherfucker had gone on to kill again, and he'd killed this sweet woman's best friend. The agony in her eyes was like a jagged blade sawing at his insides.

"Trey?"

"Mmm?"

"You know about this guy, don't you?"

His heart beat once, twice, three times. "Yes."

* * *

She waited patiently. Something was going on and she wasn't sure what.

"I've been working on the Sheldon Barnes case….I mean, I *was* working on the Sheldon Barnes case. Since he murdered Kathy Richards in San Diego about seven months ago."

She continued to gaze wordlessly at him. Dear God, he knew all about the serial killer, then. His eyes met hers, then looked away.

"I…was having some personal problems," he continued, his voice low and raspy. "And I screwed up big time. I got suspended from my job."

"Oh."

Emotions played across his face—disgust, anger, frustration. "I also… was in the hospital for a while. Then I had physical therapy. And they made me go for some counseling." He shook his head. "My suspension was up a couple of weeks ago, but I took another month's leave of absence. My plan was, like I said, to drive up to San Francisco, see my buddy Kent. We trained together at Quantico."

She put her hand to her mouth, her heart constricting. What on earth had he done that was bad enough to get him suspended? It was obviously corroding his insides like powerful acid.

"So I was taken off the case, obviously." Bitterness edged his voice. "But I know that guy." He stared across the room, past people laughing and talking and dancing, his eyes so intense she shivered. "I've studied him, talked to his family. I know that bastard better than anyone does. But I didn't know he'd killed again."

He looked back down at her. "I'm so, so sorry, Marli."

"What are you sorry for?" The corners of her eyes tightened as she looked at him and her insides squeezed at how disturbed he seemed to be by what had happened to him, and how he clearly didn't want to admit it.

He shook his head. "Marli." His voice was suddenly urgent and he settled his hands on her shoulders, holding her away from him so he could look into her eyes. Her body tensed. "Sheldon Barnes doesn't stick around after he kills someone. He's done this before and always takes off. Travels across the country. It's not likely he's still around here. And if he is, you can't be looking for him. He's a psychopath. He's dangerous."

"But—"

"Marli, you asked for my help. And here's my advice—let the police do their investigation."

She hated controlling, domineering men. At that moment, however, her body a quivery mass of stressed-out, stretched-thin nerves, she wanted to listen to this man, lean on him and let him tell her to forget about trying to find a murderer.

She was terrified. Terrified for what Krista must have endured the last moments of her life. Terrified for herself. Afraid of life without her best friend. Afraid of finding the guy and what she would do then. More afraid of not finding him.

"You don't understand," she whispered. She looked up at him, his sexy, gorgeous dark face full of concern, wavering in the tears that filled her eyes.

"What don't I understand?"

"I *have* to find him. I just have to."

He stared at her, their eyes connecting in a way she'd never experienced, like a link between them joined them, drawing them closer.

"We'll…they'll find him," he assured her urgently. "You have to believe it. But you can't do it yourself. You just can't."

"Fine." Disappointment weighed her down, her body heavy as she slid off the stool and reached for her purse. "Thanks for nothing."

He didn't even try to persuade her to stay. She looked at him for about three heartbeats, then leaned over and brushed her mouth over his.

"'Bye, Trey."

* * *

A sound downstairs caught her attention. Marli could barely hear over the noise of the water filling the tub in her bathroom. It was probably nothing. Just her stupid nerves acting up again.

But again she heard it, a grinding, grating noise coming from the lower level. Her heart stuttered to a stop, then started pounding painfully hard in her chest. She turned off the water and listened again for it. Her breath stuck in her lungs and she started slowly out of the bathroom toward the stairs, dressed in only her panties and a T-shirt. She heard it again.

"Jesus, no, no," she whimpered to herself, frozen in place at the top of the stairs, holding the chrome banister. Her fingers clenched it as her eyes darted around. Call the police, call the police, her inner voice chanted, but she was so paralyzed with fear she couldn't even remember where her phone was.

The noise stopped. She could hardly hear over the banging of her heart as she waited. A car engine roared outside, tires squealed, and then there was a pounding at her door. She jumped again, eyes in danger of popping out her sockets.

"Marli!" The voice outside called to her, but it was familiar. It was her next door neighbor, Jeff.

Her legs shook as she stumbled dangerously down the stairs and over to her front door. She pulled open the narrow blinds on the sidelight and peered out. Jeff stood there, his brows knit together, his mouth turned down. He pounded again.

"Jeff! What is it? What are you doing?"

He saw her face in the window. "Are you okay? Jesus, Marli, some guy was trying to break in your front door!"

CHAPTER 4

Marli leaned her forehead against the cold glass and gulped. Her whole body was a quivering mass of jumping nerves. With trembling hands, she unlocked the deadbolt and opened the door to let Jeff in.

He grabbed her upper arms. "Are you okay?" he demanded.

She nodded mutely, not sure if she could speak. Her knees so weak she thought she might fall, she turned out of Jeff's grasp and staggered into her living room, then collapsed on the edge of her couch.

Jeff followed her, after forcefully shutting and locking the door behind him.

"You've got to call the cops." He went into the kitchen and grabbed the cordless handset from the base, then handed it to her.

She took the phone, but did nothing. She didn't even look at Jeff, but closed her eyes.

"Marli. Call the police."

She looked at the phone and, with a curse, Jeff snatched it from her limp hand and dialed 911. She vaguely heard him report the attempted break-in through a fog of confused fear.

"Shit," he said with disgust as he hung up. "They won't come until tomorrow. You're safe, the guy's gone, it's not an emergency. Jesus."

Marli shakily pushed her hair back from her face, aware she was wearing a T-shirt and panties. Not that Jeff would notice. He was completely, openly gay. But he was a great friend and neighbor.

"Did you hear him?" she asked, finally finding her voice. "How did you…"

"I was just getting home," he said. "I guess he didn't notice me. I saw him at your door. I could tell he was trying to break in, so I yelled at him and ran over here. He took off."

"Thank you, Jeff," she said in a choked voice. "Oh, my God."

"Who was it? Any idea?"

Trey's image flashed into her head. He could have followed her home from the bar. Sure, he'd said he was a cop, but how did she know that for sure?

No. It didn't feel right. He'd been so sweetly understanding, backing off when she wanted him to, his aura of safekeeping wrapping around her.

But who else? Was it just a coincidence? A murderer was out there on the loose. "I don't know," she mumbled. "I have no idea, but I've never been so terrified. I'm a basket case as it is, then this happens." She looked up at Jeff, still standing there with the phone in his hands, looking concerned and anxious.

"You want me to stay here tonight?"

She considered that. She hated to seem weak and helpless, but damn, she was scared. "Yes," she whispered. "Would you mind?"

"Of course not. I'll sleep on your couch."

"Thank you. Do… Would you like some coffee or something?"

"Yeah. Sure."

He stayed with her while she made some tea for them, both of them knowing sleep was going to be impossible.

"Tomorrow I'm going to get an alarm system installed," she told him. "I've been so nervous ever since…"

He nodded. "That's a great idea. A single woman living alone *should* have an alarm system. You should've done that when you moved in here."

"Yeah. I should have." She *hated* feeling like this. She was a strong, independent, fun-loving woman reduced to a teeth-chattering, stuttering child.

* * *

The Super Seven Motel was cheap, but he barely had enough money for one more night, despite his new job.

He lay on the bed, staring at the ceiling in the dark.

Rage simmered in him, building and bubbling. He was not used to things being so tough for him. Marli was being difficult. It was pissing him off.

Some guy had come racing to her rescue! Jesus, after she'd been cock-teasing in the bar all night, she had another man at home. What a slut she was.

He'd been so sure she'd lived alone, didn't have a boyfriend. He narrowed his eyes.

She'd been at Cactus Jack's the last two nights in a row. Chances were good she'd be there again tonight. And so would he. He'd find a way to get her on her own.

She had to pay for what she'd done.

He imagined again how it would be. He imagined first bringing her here, to his motel room. Then he played the whole scenario through again, this time in her home. He imagined what it looked like...classy, expensive. Like her. He imagined her laughter and sneering turning to fear and disbelief. The fear in her eyes would get him going, incite him. Excitement rose in him even as he imagined it.

He'd take her first, thrust hard into her while she writhed beneath him, trying to fight him off. He knew she would try to fight, and he could already feel the adrenaline rush of controlling her. He'd hurt her...slap her, punch her...his imagination roamed for different ways to inflict pain on her. He'd enjoy every minute of her luscious terror, her screaming and begging him to stop. She would be one he'd need to tie up. He smiled.

He'd make her sorry she'd laughed at him, mocked him for being a cowboy. She'd be sorry she walked away from him.

Then he'd kill her.

* * *

Marli had to beg the alarm company to come that day, and the tears making her voice wobbly weren't forced when she told them about the attempted break-in the night before. She waited at home all day, doors locked, blinds closed. She'd had to cancel a shoot, rescheduling it for next week, and the client was not happy.

She tried to focus on work in her home office, invoicing and doing her books, the part of owning her own business that she hated. Not only was she jolted by every little noise she heard—every car that pulled up on the street, every creak, even the refrigerator motor going on and off—but thoughts of Trey kept tugging her thoughts away from her work. She recalled the humor in his eyes as they talked and laughed, the way he'd looked at her with hot desire he was keeping carefully banked because he knew she was nervous.

Was she going to go back to Cactus Jack's tonight?

He'd told her not to. He'd told her to forget about that crazy idea and let the cops deal with it. But he didn't understand. He didn't understand how the guilt was eating away at her. She couldn't even say the words out loud, admit to someone else that she was responsible for her friend's death. That was just too hard, too horrendous. It was…unspeakable.

She had to go. For Krista.

* * *

He wasn't there.

Marli found a seat at the bar, but it wasn't where she preferred to sit. She was later getting there than the other evenings and almost every stool at the bar was taken. Oh, well, she could move later.

She gazed around, sipping her Diet Coke. Trey had, no doubt, gone on to San Francisco. He wasn't willing to help her and, although they both knew they were attracted to each other, she'd made it pretty clear to him she had no intention on acting on the attraction, so he'd probably just moved on.

She had other more important things to worry about. Again, her eyes scanned the crowds, stopping on every big, blond man there to study him. Disappointment and anxiety battled within her.

With a sigh, she looked down at her drink. It was going to be a long evening.

She watched people come and go, politely refused offers of drinks and invitations to dance, sitting there by herself on her barstool. By midnight, she'd had enough. She left a tip for the bartender who'd brought her the single Diet Coke she'd drank all evening and snagged her purse from where it hung on the back of the stool.

Outside the bar, the dark chill of evening shrouded her. She hugged her purse close and wrapped her arms around herself as she walked to her car in the parking garage. The attendant on duty in his little lit-up booth read a magazine. Were there security cameras? She made sure to walk by him so he'd know she was going to her car, just in case. But her car was up two levels and she had to take the stairs to get there.

She dreaded going into the stairwell. Why was she doing this to herself? She pulled open the door and stepped in. It was well-lit, which helped a little, but even so she ran up the stairs as fast as she could, bursting out of the door into the dimly lit parking structure. There weren't many cars on this level. She headed straight to hers, her keys ready.

She heard the door behind her. Someone else had come onto this level. *It's okay. It's okay.* Just someone else going to his vehicle. She wanted to look, but focused on walking to her car as quickly as she could.

A hand yanked her back. Her heart leaped into her throat and she cried out as arms encircled her from behind in a lung-squeezing grip.

CHAPTER 5

Marli's heart galloped wildly in her chest. She gave a choked gasp, instinctively dug her fingers into the arms and tried to pry them off her. She opened her mouth, tried to scream as loud as she could, raw sound scraping over her throat as she struggled furiously against the power of his restraining arms. *Oh, Jesus, no, no!* She couldn't breathe. Her keys were in her hand, but she couldn't get them into position to use them. She was going to die. Or was he going to rape her? Oh, God, this could not be happening.

"Here," she squawked. "My purse…" If he wanted money, he could have money. But he knocked the purse to the ground without releasing her and dragged her toward the stairwell.

You weren't supposed to fight. You were just supposed to give them the money. But he didn't want money. *Oh, God.*

She was not going to die without a fight. Krista had fought.

She tried to dig her heels into the concrete, but they just scraped across it as he pulled her. A strangled cry escaped her. The man grunted as he tried to avoid her flailing arms and kicking feet, but he was stronger than she was. He said nothing, just yanked at her. Pain seared from her shoulder down her arm, and she cried out again. She fought harder, with frantic energy, crying out with pain and effort and fear.

"Hey!"

Someone else was there. Was he there to help her—or to help the mugger?

An even bigger man dragged the attacker off her, and with an impressive swing, crunched the guy's jaw. Her attacker staggered back a step, making a rough sound. The other man drew back to hit again. The mugger swung an arm up, broke the other's grip on his jacket, turned and fled, his uneven footsteps echoing in the garage.

"Marli, are you okay?" Trey stood in front of her.

She gasped for breath, standing there in stunned disbelief.

"Should I go after him?"

She shook her head. *Yes. No. God.* The adrenaline shooting through her veins made her weak and dizzy.

He grabbed her shoulders. "Marli? Did he hurt you?"

She just kept staring, wide-eyed, a quivering mass of nerves, everything dark and twirling around her.

"I'm..." Her knees started to buckle, and Trey caught her.

"Shit, Marli." He held her up against his big, warm body. "Where are you hurt? Should I take you to the hospital?" One handed lifted her chin to see her face. "Marli! Talk to me."

"I'm not hurt," she managed to mumble. "I'm...okay."

She wasn't okay. She was a mess. Her arm throbbed, her stomach tossed and she thought she might throw up or pass out. She put a hand to her mouth. Her stomach heaved and her mouth filled with saliva.

"Jesus." He turned her away from him, held her hips as she bent over and retched painfully, empting her stomach onto the concrete floor of the garage.

She felt him fumbling, then he had a cell phone and was calling the police.

"Don't even bother," she said weakly, eyes closed against the sight of her vomit on the floor, still bent over. "They won't do anything." She rubbed cold, sweaty palms over her face.

Yes, they will." She listened to him report the incident in a calm, professional tone. Then he handed to phone to her. "You're going to have to talk to them. They need details from you that I don't know. Your last name, address..."

She took the phone, and somehow he was handing her a crumpled tissue he'd pulled from his jacket pocket. She wiped first her eyes, wet from watering while she'd heaved her guts out, then her mouth. She spoke to the police, trying to remember her own name and address.

When she was done, she carefully flipped his phone closed and handed it back to him.

"I have to go in tomorrow to make a statement," she said. "I told you not to bother. It was the same last night."

"What happened last night?" he asked sharply.

She pushed her hair back wearily. "I want to go home," she said, her voice small and despicably quavery.

"I'll take you home." His voice was rough. "Where's your car?"

She pointed to her Sebring convertible. "I almost made it," she said sadly, letting him lead her to the car. "I was so afraid…"

He tried to put her in the passenger seat, but she resisted. "No! You're not coming with me."

"Yes, I am."

This time he wasn't letting her push him away. It should have scared her, but instead she wanted to let him take charge, let him look after her.

"No," she protested again, this time more weakly. "I can't go home with a stranger. I don't even know you."

"Marli, I'm a cop. Some guy just jumped you. I'm coming with you."

She stared into his eyes. How did she know he was really a cop? But the intensity and power of his gaze comforted her. She swallowed hard, still shaking. For a long moment, thoughts ran through her head, one crazy idea chasing another until finally she knew she had to listen to her instincts. While her brain kept saying no, for a million rational reasons, her heart was telling her this man was solid and trustworthy.

"Okay." She slumped into the passenger seat. When he went around and got into the driver's seat, he leaned over and did her seatbelt up for her. Then he adjusted the driver's seat, pushing it back as far as it would go to allow for his long legs.

When he got to the exit, the gate was up and the parking lot attendant wasn't there. Trey barely slowed to leave, and Marli wasn't going to remind him that they were supposed to pay.

She huddled in the seat, shivering, her insides cold and shaking. Trey kept glancing at her, his brows lowered over his deep-set eyes, giving him a powerfully intimidating look. She managed to choke out directions to her home, and he pulled into the driveway moments later.

When they walked in, the alarm system she'd just had installed hours ago started beeping and she stared helplessly at the control panel. For the life of her, she could not remember the code. She glanced at Trey, confused.

"The code, Marli? The code?"

Beep. Beep. Beep.

She nodded, biting her lip. "I can't remember it," she whispered.

"Um…" She punched in a number, her fingers trembling so badly she missed the number. The beeping continued, making her shake even harder. "Shit." She tried again. This time, the beeping stopped and she fell against the wall, weak with relief.

"Christ, Marli." Trey kicked the door shut behind them, scooped her up and carried her into the house.

"Lock the door," she said, teeth chattering, as he lowered her onto the couch.

He obediently turned around and went back to lock the door and the deadbolt.

"And put the alarm on again," she called out to him. She heard him stop, hoping he knew which button, then he appeared around the corner.

He sat down on the couch beside her and pulled her into his arms. They sat like that for a long time, while he cuddled her and stroked her hair. She swallowed hard through a tight throat, eyes stinging, breathing tightly. But then, hot and helpless tears overflowed and, to her shame, she found herself sobbing into Trey's shoulder. He held her, pressed his cheek against her hair, letting her cry, big heaving sobs that left her exhausted, drained.

He found her box of tissues on the end table and handed her some so she could mop herself up. She sat up, not wanting to look at him. She could imagine what a mess she was. She was so deeply embarrassed to have cried in front of him. She never cried. Only in front of Krista. She closed her eyes against the wave of pain that thought brought.

"What happened last night, Marli?"

* * *

"That smoke break was a little long, there, Sam." Laura scowled at him.

He smiled. "Sorry, Laura. I tried to squeeze in two."

"What happened to your face?" She looked closer at him, but he waved her away.

"I was rushing back and I opened the door right into my chin," he told her. "I'm fine."

"Okay," she said, looking doubtfully at him. "Get back to work."

He saluted her and winked, and she gave him a reluctant smile.

Women. They were so stupid; he could get them to do anything.

When her back was turned, his smile disappeared. *Fuck!* Nothing was going right for him lately. He slammed a hand against the wall, frustration and anger simmering inside him. Once again, she'd gotten away from him. He didn't know who the hell the bastard was who'd jumped him from behind, but he was betting it was that bozo who'd been all over her last night.

He cursed again under his breath as he went back to work. But at least he knew where she lived. Earlier today, before he'd started work, he'd gone by her place, but the damn cops had been there, so he'd just kept going. Soon as he finished work, he'd head over there again. This time he'd use the back door.

CHAPTER 6

She still wouldn't look at him, and Trey shifted on the couch beside her, turning her, lifting her face gently with his fingers beneath her chin. She was a mess, but still gorgeous. Those green and gold eyes shimmered wetly, still wide with fear. Her long lashes fluttered as she closed her eyes rather than meet his gaze.

He rubbed at a smear of mascara under one eye with his thumb. Both hands framed her face and he leaned in and brushed his mouth across hers.

"Come on, Marli. You have to tell me now."

"How did you…why were you there? Tonight?"

He sighed and his mouth twisted. That guilt stabbed through him again. "I had every intention of leaving today, but I couldn't stand the idea of you going back there alone looking for a psychopathic serial killer. Jesus." He shook his head. "I saw you going into the parking garage. I was in my car. I had to find a place to park, and then I followed you."

"Did you see…"

"No, but I was in there when I heard you scream. Jesus Christ. I never—" He stopped, shook his head. "I could not fucking believe it when I saw that guy on you. Fuck." His stomach cramped at the memory. The fear and rage he'd experienced had astonished him. He barely knew this girl. Was it just his training kicking in?

"What happened last night?" he asked again, cupping her face in both hands.

She sighed and looked down at her fingers twisting together in her lap. Then she sat up straighter and squared her shoulders. "Someone tried to break in here. Just after I got home."

He sucked in a breath. This was insane.

"My next door neighbor came home and scared him away before he got in. I heard the noise, though." Her voice broke and she struggled for control for a moment.

He waited. He could wait forever.

"We called the police and they wouldn't even come. Because I was okay and Jeff was there and the guy never got in. They came today, but they barely even looked at my door. So, I got an alarm system installed."

Thank Christ for that. He'd noticed all the lights blazing in her home when he'd pulled into the driveway, wondering if she lived with someone else.

"Do you live here alone?"

She glanced at him and hesitated.

"You're safe with me, Marli," he said, reading her apprehension.

She nodded. "Yes. I live alone. Jeff said I should've had an alarm system a long time ago."

"Jeff?" The little sting of jealousy again surprised him.

"My neighbor. He stayed with me last night so I wouldn't be alone."

He nodded, pushing the jealousy aside. "And then tonight some guy attacks you."He covered her restless hands with his, separated her fingers, twined them with his and held them still. Hers were small and icy-cold beneath his as his fingers closed around hers.

"Do you…do you think it was him?"

He bent his head. "Hell, I don't know. It isn't usually the way he works. Your friend Krista…*that's* the way he works. He meets women in bars, smooth talks them, buys them drinks, leaves with them…and kills them."

His harsh words made her flinch.

"You're in shock," he told her. "Your hands are freezing, your teeth keep chattering, your pupils are dilated. I don't know how you're holding it together." He took her hands in his and stood up, pulling her with him. "Let's get you to bed."

* * *

Even in her state of near collapse, a flare of heat sparked inside her at his words. She still felt that sexual pull, the heat between them.

"Sleep," he said, apparently reading her mind. "You need sleep."

"I can't sleep," she protested as he started leading her to the stairs.

"I assume your bedroom is up here?" he asked, ignoring her.

She nodded.

"Have you got any drugs? Sleeping pills?"

"No! Of course not."

"It's not that bad." He pulled her up the staircase. "After someone's been through what you have, a doctor will often prescribe a mild sedative for sleep. You need to sleep."

Yeah, that might have been a good idea, in hindsight, she thought. The lack of sleep for the last few weeks was probably making her irrational, more emotional and sensitive than she needed to be. She followed along behind him, content to let him take charge, too tired and weak to fight it.

"How about booze?" he asked, walking into her bedroom.

She saw him looking around, taking it in. She bit her lip as she noticed the clothes strewn over the chair in the corner, the shoes kicked off and laying on the carpet, the pile of books on the floor beside the bed. She wished she were a neater person.

"I know you weren't drinking at the bar…does that mean you don't drink at all? Or do you have a bottle of wine or whiskey or something here somewhere?"

"Um…" Her mind was a bit foggy. "I have tequila." She frowned. The last time she'd drank tequila was when this whole mess had started. If she and Krista hadn't argued that night…

"I'll get you some. Where is it?"

"No. I don't want tequila. There's a bottle of wine in the fridge."

"Okay. You get into bed. I'll be back in a minute."

She went into the bathroom, gazed longingly at her big Jacuzzi tub. Probably not a good idea with Trey here, but after he left, she'd have a long, hot soak. That would relax her.

She peeled off the denim jacket she wore, then the long silk and lace camisole under it. She washed her face mindlessly, scrubbing away the mascara smeared under her eyes, making her nose even pinker. Then she wriggled out of her snug jeans and walked back into her bedroom in her bra and panties, just as Trey entered with a glass of wine.

His eyes moved over her, then went dark and hot. Her mouth went dry. Her nipples tingled. *Jeez.* How could she be having an attack of lust at a time like this, after what had just happened to her?

"Get into bed," he ordered roughly. He followed her, arranged pillows behind her so she was propped up, then handed her the glass of wine. He sat down at the end of her bed, far, far away from her. "Drink that," he said. "Then try to get some sleep."

"Yes, sir," she snipped. Then she softened. "Um…thank you Trey. I didn't say it earlier, but thank you for coming along when you did and rescuing me. I'm really, really grateful." God, what would have happened if he hadn't come? He'd probably saved her life. Her chest constricted painfully.

He nodded shortly.

"Are you going to San Francisco tomorrow?"

He frowned. "Hell, no."

"Why not?"

He passed a hand over his face. His dark shadow of a beard was prominent, this late in the day…or rather, this early in the morning. It was after two o'clock. He, too, looked weary. "I'm going to talk to the cops tomorrow," he said. "I don't know if they've made the connection between your break-in and the attack tonight and the fact that Sheldon Barnes knows you."

His words reminded her of what deep shit she was in, and she gulped the wine.

"They need to know he may have changed his appearance," he told her. "And that he may be still here in the LA area."

She nodded. Then she carefully set the wine glass down on her bedside table. "I'll see you out," she said quietly. "So I can lock up behind you. And I'll need to disarm the alarm so you can get out."

He just looked at her. "I'm not going anywhere. I'll sleep on your couch. I'm not leaving you here alone."

"That's why I got the alarm," she protested. "You don't have to stay."

"I'm staying."

They stared at each other for a long moment.

"Fine," she huffed out, flopping back on the pillows. "But you'll have to sleep on the couch. My spare bedroom is an office."

"I can sleep on the couch. Just tell me where I can find a pillow and a blanket."

She started to get out of bed, but he pushed her back down without much apparent effort on his part. "I'll find it," he said mildly. "Just tell me where."

"But—"

"You are one stubborn, independent woman," he marveled. "Is it that you don't like *me* telling you what to do? Or are you just ornery?"

She glared at him. "Both," she snapped.

He grinned. She couldn't help but smile back and suddenly she was reliving how exciting and fun flirting with him had been. Awareness that they were alone in her bedroom and she was dressed only in her skimpy underwear hit her low in the belly.

Warmth slid over her, starting in her cheeks, down over her throat and chest, and she slowly pulled the duvet up under her chin, pressing back into the pillow.

"Don't worry, Marli." He touched her cheek, then stroked a strand of hair back off her face. "You know I'd love nothing more than to get in that bed with you, but this is not the time. I know that."

She nodded, eyes still fastened on his. "I know," she whispered. "But if it wasn't a bad time, I'd love it, too."

His eyes darkened. "God, you shouldn't say things like that."

"Oh, Jesus, I know." She closed her eyes. "I can't help it. I just say things. And it comes across all wrong."

"And what was the *right* way for that comment to come across?"

When she opened her eyes, she saw his face still tight with control, but one brow was raised and humor glimmered in his dark eyes. She smiled slowly back at him.

His fingers continued to stroke her hair back from her face and it was so sexy, yet soothing, warm sensation sliding over her. Her eyes drooped with fatigue. "There are blankets and a pillow in the closet in my office. The room next door." She yawned. "I'm sorry…I feel I should get it for you."

He touched her mouth, smiling at her yawn. "I can find it. Go to sleep. You must be wiped."

He turned out the lamp beside her bed and left the room quietly. She could hear him in the room next door, getting things out of the closet. When he walked by her door, she called out.

"Trey?"

He stopped in the doorway, his big body a dark, solid silhouette. Reassuring.

"Could you leave my door open a little wider? And leave the hall light on?"

He nodded and pushed the door open. She heard his heavy steps going down to the living room and then she closed her eyes and drifted into sleep.

She might have been asleep for two hours or two minutes when a loud wailing noise pierced her consciousness. For a moment, she tried to figure out what it was. Then her heart jumped into her throat and she bolted up in bed.

Her new alarm was going off.

CHAPTER 7

What the... She pushed her hair back from her face and held her head. Then she remembered.

"Trey!" She scrambled out from under the covers, terror gripping her in a frigid clasp. He was down there. She dashed out of the room, oblivious to the fact she was half-naked. In her haste, her bare foot snagged on the carpet and she tripped. She grabbed the railing, caught herself, hair falling in her face, then stumbled down the rest of the stairs.

The front door was still secure. Blankets were in a heap on the floor and Trey was nowhere to be seen. Her glance ricocheted around the room, then she lurched into her kitchen. The back door stood open, the cool night air blowing in and raising goose bumps on her bare skin. She ran to the door and grabbed it, using it to hold herself up, her legs shaky, knees weak.

"God, no," she whimpered looking out into the darkness. Frantically she searched her small dark yard for Trey, but saw nothing. "Oh. Oh, no."

She grabbed the cordless phone off the charger on the counter and, with fingers shaking almost uncontrollably, she punched in 911, running back out onto her deck to scan the yard. She was gasping out answers to the operator's calm questions when Trey appeared on the steps of the deck.

"Son of a bitch." He bent at the waist, panting. "He got away." He lifted his head and looked at her. "Get back in the house, for God's sake. You have no clothes on."

She looked down at herself, then back at him. "Who cares? Jesus, you're bossy."

"Marli, someone just tried to break into your house. Again. Listen to me."

She backed up, and he came toward her, slamming the door shut behind him. It bounced open again. The lock had been damaged so it wouldn't close. "Shit," he muttered.

The alarm was still wailing. "Is it connected to the police?" he asked as she scurried to the control panel.

"Yes. I already called them." She punched in the code, this time remembering it, and silence descended.

She looked at Trey as she hung up the phone. "I can't believe this," she whispered. She covered her face with her hands. "I just cannot believe this."

He walked over to her and wrapped his arms around her. "God, Marli, it's okay. You're okay, and I'm here. And I'm not leaving. I don't care what you say."

That was fine with her. She might have protested earlier, but now? No way. He could stay forever.

"After the cops come, I'm going to nail the door shut for tonight," he said. "We'll get you a new door tomorrow. And on second thought, I'm not staying here tonight."

Her heart dropped to her toes. "You're…you're not?"

He shook his head. "And neither are you. I'm taking you back to my hotel with me. Even with an alarm this place isn't safe."

"He won't try again tonight. He can't be that stupid." She was afraid even to think about going to Trey's hotel room with him.

"No, he's not stupid," he agreed. "And he likely won't try again tonight. Even so, we're leaving. Get dressed."

Man, he liked to give orders. Funny, she'd never noticed that about him when they'd been talking and laughing at Cactus Jack's. But put the man in a crime scene and he was spouting commands and orders all over the place. She did what he said, though, his forceful, self-assured presence only adding to the sense of security she felt with him.

* * *

Trey dealt with the police, boarded her back door shut, and then carried the small duffel bag she'd packed for the night out to her car.

He drove back to Cactus Jack's. The neon sign was dark, the bar closed.

"What are we doing here?" she asked.

"Getting my vehicle. Barnes probably knows your car, so I don't want to take it to the hotel."

He parked her car on the street in front of his, and they got into his car and drove the few blocks to the Rocky Harbor Inn. They walked through the deserted lobby to the elevators.

They rode up in silence. He was intensely aware of her in the elevator, images of her in her white lace bra and panties flashing through his mind. Diamonds flashing in the shallow indentation of her navel. *Jesus.* That was not where his mind should be right now. There was a lunatic killer after her. And it was his fault.

He slid his key card in and out and shoved down on the lever to open the door. He hit the switch on the wall and a lamp illuminated the dark space.

The king-size bed dominated the room, but a small, nicely furnished sitting area occupied a corner in front of the floor-to-ceiling window. Sliding doors opened onto a small balcony looking out over the Pacific Ocean. Fronds of a palm tree swayed just next to the second-floor balcony railing.

The sky was the deep, intense dark blue that preceded dawn. *Man, what a night.*

He turned to Marli, dropping her bag onto the dresser. He moved over to her.

"You're amazing," he said. She'd been through worse than he had and was still standing. She was pale and kept swallowing convulsively, but she was hanging in there.

"No, I'm not," she whispered.

When he touched his mouth to hers, she looked up at him with huge eyes, their sparkle dimmed by fatigue.

"We both need to get some sleep." He unzipped her black hoodie sweatshirt and pushed it off her shoulders. Underneath, she wore a thin ribbed white tank, the lacy cups of her bra clearly visible through it. He sucked in a breath, trying to remember that sleep was the goal.

He looked down and his fingers undid the drawstring tie of her black yoga pants, sitting low on her hips. Then he slid a finger inside them, tugging them looser until they dropped to the floor.

He reached down and yanked back the covers of the bed so she could crawl in. To his surprise, she did so without arguing with him, for once. Man, she was one determined lady. She should be a sniveling heap on the floor, yet she still stood up to him when he tried to tell her what to do. He couldn't help but smile.

"What's so funny?" she murmured, as she settled her head into the pillow.

"You are." He tucked the blankets around her. "You're awesome."

"Oh. Okay." Her eyes were drifting closed already. "Tell me more about that later."

Still smiling, he went and hung the "Do Not Disturb" sign on the outside of the door and flipped the security lock into place. Then he shed his own clothes and slid naked under the covers.

Remarkably, Marli's breathing had slowed, telling him she was asleep. She must have been exhausted. So was he, but having her next to him in the bed, the warmth of her body, the soft sounds of her breathing, was making him so horny he doubted sleep would be possible.

* * *

Trey woke up long before Marli did. For a while, he lay there watching her sleep.

She fascinated him. His eyes moved over her hair, so bright and shiny, long coils spread around her face on the pillow. He lifted one curl from her face and placed it behind her. Eyebrows and long, long eyelashes a darker shade of gold framed her eyes. Her skin was impossibly smooth and creamy. She was obviously not the typical California golden girl who baked in the sun. She lay on her side facing him and one slim shoulder curved out from beneath the covers, the thin strap of her bra slipping down. Her breast was falling out of the cup, the smooth, full curve enticing, the nipple almost revealed. With one finger, he could edge the cup back a little more and see all of her, but he resisted, determined to let her get as much sleep as she could.

A little mole marked her chest, just at the edge of her right breast, which he also longed to touch. He sighed. He was a patient man. He could wait hours at a hostage situation, question witnesses with endless endurance, pore over investigation material at length, but he found himself impatient for Marli.

He slid out of the bed and rummaged in his suitcase for clean underwear. He pulled on a pair of black boxer briefs, then a pair of baggy cargo shorts. He didn't bother with a shirt.

He found his laptop, plugged in to the high-speed internet connection provided by the hotel and booted it up. He started surfing the net, searching for news stories of Sheldon Barnes.

He learned as much as he could about the most recent murder, but he really needed to talk to the feds. He sighed. His suspension was over. Now he was on vacation, so maybe they'd talk to him.

As he surfed the net and read, he couldn't help but think about the night his life had all gone to shit. The night he'd let Sheldon Barnes walk out of that bar.

The woman Sheldon had been with that night had gotten lucky. She'd somehow convinced Sheldon to stop at a store so she could use the bathroom and had run like hell out the back door.

But Krista Mackie hadn't been so lucky.

Every murder victim touched something inside Trey, but he'd learned over the years to shut off that part of him. He couldn't do his job if emotion distracted him. But knowing Krista was Marli's best friend and seeing the pain in Marli's face made him able to clearly imagine the last moments of Krista's life.

Guilt ate at him. Marli's friend would still be alive if he hadn't been wallowing in self-pity that night at the Pinto Club. He hadn't told Marli that part yet. He *so* did not want to tell her that part.

He sighed.

Marli stirred in the bed, and he glanced over at her. Her eyes flickered open. She looked so different without mascara on those gold eyelashes. Softer…vulnerable. He smiled at her and she smiled back.

"Hey," he said softly, "you're awake."

"Yeah." She pulled the covers up under her chin and stayed there.

He wondered if she was shy about getting out of bed with him there. "Do you want me to…uh…go out on the balcony?"

She stared at him blankly for a moment, then laughed. "God, no." She threw back the covers and swung her long, long legs over the side of the bed. She sat there, hands on the edge of the mattress, leaning forward. "How long have you been awake?"

"Couple of hours. Do you feel better?"

She nodded and pushed a hand through her hair, ruffling it in an attempt to smooth the tangled curls. She yawned and stood up.

He hadn't had a chance to fully appreciate her body last night, or this morning. She was all long, lean muscles under smooth skin, slim-waisted, full-breasted. His eyes were drawn helplessly to those sparkly jewels piercing her navel. When she walked toward the bathroom, the long muscles in her thighs flexed, and the view from behind as she walked away was just as outstanding. Tiny lace panties barely covered firm, rounded cheeks.

He gulped. He had to keep her here, but it could be problematic sharing a hotel room and keeping his hands off her.

She grabbed her bag as she went into the bathroom. He heard water running, the toilet flushing. Then she reappeared, still clad only in bra and panties. So much for shyness.

She sat back down on the bed and looked at him. "So? How long are you going to keep me here?"

"You're not a prisoner."

She laughed. "I'm kidding. Believe me, if I want to leave, I'll leave."

He had no doubt of that. She seemed to have recovered from the traumatic events of the previous day.

"It so happens I'm feeling in need of protection right now," she said lightly. "So I'm in no hurry to leave."

"Oh. Okay. Good."

"I am hungry, though."

Hell. He hadn't even thought about food. Now that she said it, though, he realized he was ravenous, too. He reached for the room service menu and handed it to her.

She opened it up and flipped the pages. "Waffles." She snapped it closed and handed it back to him. "Orange juice and coffee. Lots of coffee."

He grinned and picked up the phone. He added bacon, eggs, pancakes, sausages and toast for himself.

When he hung up, he looked back at her. "Uh…are you going to get dressed?"

She shot him a sultry smile. "Am I bothering you?"

His lips curved up in response. "Hell, yeah."

Her smile widened, but she stood up and searched the room for her clothes. "I put your stuff in the closet," he told her. She looked like a damn supermodel as she strode on those long legs to the closet. She pulled on the same yoga pants and tank top she'd been wearing when they arrived, leaving off the hoodie for now.

Somehow, even though she was dressed, it didn't help take his attention away from her. The tank hugged her breasts and left a strip of smooth flesh bare between its hem and the low-riding drawstring of the pants. Fortunately, room service provided a distraction by delivering their food.

He put away his laptop, and they spread their breakfast feast across the table, pulling up two chairs. Marli poured them each a cup of coffee from the thermos, adding cream and sugar to hers. She topped her waffle with all the whipped butter and then looked at his.

"What?" he asked.

"Are you going to use that butter?"

He looked down at his pancakes. "Yeah."

"Oh." She shrugged her slim shoulders, and, before he even knew he was doing it, he picked up the little container of butter and handed it over. She rewarded him with a radiant smile. He shook his head.

"I thought *I* had a big appetite," she said, indicating the plates full of food in front of him.

He laughed. "I lost some weight after…a while ago. I'm still trying to get back up to fighting weight."

She looked at him with frank appreciation. "You look good."

He flashed back to the night they'd met at Cactus Jack's. She'd said that then, too. That night, he hadn't been sure how to take that comment. Today, the warm admiration in her eyes left him no doubt.

Warmth spread from his chest downward. He ducked his head and started cutting his pancakes. When he looked up at her, she was smiling.

"Marli…"

"What?" She looked at him with innocent eyes and slowly put a piece of waffle into her mouth with her fork.

"Are you flirting with me?"

And just like that, her gaze shuttered. *Shit.* "What?" he asked, confused. "What did I say?"

She put down her knife and fork and stared at her plate. Then she looked back up at him, her lips firming, eyes clear. "Yes," she said. "I guess I was flirting with you. I'm sorry."

"Jesus, don't apologize! I'm not complaining. I just wanted to be clear…because, if you're flirting with me, you'd better be prepared for what might happen."

CHAPTER 8

"What might happen?" Her voice came out husky.

She watched his Adam's apple bob as he swallowed hard. He looked back at her, clearly debating how to answer. When he spoke, his voice was low, rough. "I might rip all your clothes off and fuck your brains out."

His reply shocked her, thrilled her, but she smiled, still watching him. "I might not mind that," she said softly.

Their eyes met and held across the table, sexual tension rising in her until she ached with need. Then he shook his head. "Finish your breakfast."

She kept smiling, but turned her attention back to her food. She was starving and it felt good to be hungry for a change. She, too, hadn't been eating much lately. Although, despite her appetite, she found she actually couldn't eat as much as she wanted to. She had to leave some of the huge Belgian waffle untouched. She sipped her coffee and watched Trey devour his own food.

When he'd cleaned every plate and leaned back in his chair, she grinned.

"Feel better?"

He smiled back at her. "Yeah. That was good."

"So, what's the plan now?"

Trey glanced at his watch. "I'm going to make a couple of calls, then I'm going to the FBI office in LA. You can wait here."

"Uh-uh. I'm not staying here alone."

"You'll be safe here." Although he didn't appear entirely convinced of that when he eyed the sliding glass door. They were only on the second floor, which was not difficult to access. "Okay, you can come with me."

"Can I have a shower first?"

"Sure. I wouldn't mind a shower, too."

She looked at him and she knew he could tell what she was thinking.

"Go," he said, pointing at the bathroom.

Grinning, she helped pile their dishes back onto the tray and tossed garbage into the wastebasket.

She showered and shampooed her hair, the hot water pummeling her body like a massage therapist, easing out tension and knots. She stayed under the spray for long moments, trying to let her stress swirl down the drain along with the foamy shampoo suds. She used the hotel hair dryer to dry her hair partially, but her curls dried better if she just left them alone. She'd packed so quickly she didn't have her anti-frizz serum with her, so she ran conditioner through her damp hair and hoped for the best.

She swiped eye shadow onto her lids, brushed mascara over her pale lashes, and slicked gloss over her lips. Just that made her feel a little better as she gazed at her reflection in the steamy mirror.

She took a deep, shaky breath. She was okay. She was here, she was alive, and she was with Trey. She barely knew him, but she felt safe with him.

Not that she needed a man. She could look after herself. But damn, it felt so good to have him there.

And not just for protection. Watching him sit at the table in front of his laptop, she'd studied his chest and shoulders. He said he'd lost weight, but he was still impressively muscled, his shoulders thick, biceps rounded, his pecs and abs well-defined. He had just enough dark body hair to look masculine, but not gorilla-like.

He still hadn't shaved and his dark beard gave him a dangerous look, along with those deep-set, intense eyes. Intelligent eyes, which had roved over the computer screen quickly, reading and absorbing information.

She was *so* attracted to him. She was trying not to flirt, but apparently, she just couldn't help it. Even innocent remarks came out wrong. But the electricity sparking between them, the heat, that intense pull, almost made her forget she was *not* supposed to be having fun.

She was supposed to be miserable and grieving, being punished for her sins.

She went back into the room where Trey still sat with his laptop and cell phone. He was talking to someone named Bill and scribbling notes, focused and intent, and sexy as hell.

She threw the covers up in a half-hearted attempt to make the bed. Then she wandered to the window and gazed out at the ocean, blinding and blue, the sky dotted with puffy white clouds zipping along. It must be windy.

She sighed and turned back to the room, restless and edgy. She spotted a familiar magazine provided by the hotel, advertising Rocky Harbor attractions, and grabbed it off the desk. She flopped onto the bed on her stomach, facing Trey, her feet in the air, and flipped through it while he talked.

"Okay," he said, sounding like he was wrapping up. "Thanks, man. I'm going over there now. Yeah, yeah, I'll keep you posted." He snapped his phone shut and looked at Marli.

She gazed back at him inquiringly.

"That was my partner, Bill Patterson," he said. "Former partner." A note of bitterness crept into his voice. "He gave me contact names at the LA bureau."

She nodded.

Trey stood. "I'm going to have a quick shower."

She nodded again, watched him walk into the bathroom. God, he was gorgeous. She wanted to run her hands over the smooth skin and muscle, feel how hard he was. A throbbing ache started between her legs, and she rolled onto her back and stared at the ceiling.

She pictured him naked in the shower. He'd seen her practically naked, but all she'd seen was his chest. Although his chest was delicious enough to make her mouth water. Her breasts swelled a little, nipples tight. She closed her eyes. A flood of longing wet her panties.

He was probably soaping his body up now. She knew his thighs were big, could tell from the jeans he'd worn. God, she wanted to see them, to see where they joined his hips, his groin…

With a moan, she rolled back onto her stomach and pressed her hot face into the silky cool bedspread. Her pelvis pushed into the bed instinctively. She was still lying like that, trying to control the throbbing heat, when Trey flung open the bathroom and emerged in a cloud of steam, clad only in his underwear.

She peeked at him through a veil of hair without lifting her head, watching him rummage through his suitcase wearing only a pair of snug black boxer briefs.

Oh, yeah. His thighs *were* big. His ass was tight. Muscles rippled as he pulled on a pair of black dress pants and the white shirt he'd been wearing the night they met. This time he tucked it in and added a sleek leather belt to the pants.

When he was dressed, she lifted her head. "You look very professional," she told him. "Very hot, but very professional."

Why had she said that? Why, why, why?

His cheeks flushed a little as he finished buckling the belt, then shoved his hands into the pockets.

"Hey, look," she said, rolling off the bed. She grabbed the magazine and moved over beside him. "Nice photo, huh?"

She folded the magazine open and displayed a glossy page advertising a local restaurant.

He looked at the photo, then at her face. "Yours?" he guessed.

She nodded, smiling. She flipped a few pages. "And this one. And…this one."

The last was a full-page advertisement for Surf Coast Brewery, featuring a huge golden dog smiling and…winking.

He grinned. "How did you get the dog to wink?"

"I winked at him…like this…" She demonstrated. "And he winked back."

Trey laughed. "Bullshit."

She laughed, too. "Okay, it was Photoshop." She studied the image. "I did a damn fine job if I do say so myself."

He looked at it again and nodded. "It looks so real." He smiled at her. "I don't know much about photography, but you're obviously good."

His compliment made her feel good. Warm. Almost happy.

Except she wasn't allowed to be happy. Her mood sank like a brick in water.

"You ready?" He grabbed his wallet, cell phone and the papers he'd scribbled notes on.

"You betcha." She picked up her purse, a big soft brown leather sack, and slung it over her shoulder. She took a deep breath. Leaving the sanctuary of Trey's hotel room was just a little scary.

Fear, however, seemed silly as they walked through the busy, bright lobby of the hotel and out into the parking lot. The sun hurt her eyes, the breeze tossed the fronds of the palm trees lining the front of the hotel and clouds scudded across the sky. The world seemed so impossibly normal.

They hit the 405, exiting a while later onto Wilshire to find the federal office building where the FBI field office was located.

"Have you been here before?" she asked him.

"Yeah. Lots of times." He parked.

They rode up the elevator.

"You can wait over there." Trey nodded to a small lounge area, going over to a security desk.

"Okay."

She wandered over. The chairs were hard chrome and vinyl, and she glanced at some ancient *Time* magazines. Trey disappeared down an aisle between cubicles, and she heard his voice as he greeted his colleagues and they started talking.

She sighed. They were talking about her. At least, some of it was about her. She took little comfort from being in the offices of the FBI. They sure hadn't done anything to protect her. If it weren't for Trey… Her teeth dug into her bottom lip.

An hour later Trey was still in there talking. She tossed the last *Time* magazine down and sighed. Tapped her fingers on the armrest of the chair. Shifted her rapidly numbing butt. What the hell was taking so long? Then she was annoyed with herself. He was trying to help her after all.

When Trey finally emerged, she jumped up and crossed over to him, so happy to see his face. She'd known the man for three days and already he was her anchor. Two other men in bad suits accompanied him.

Trey introduced her and they shook her hand. Trey didn't look all that happy. She looked from his face to the other men and back. Then he was hustling her out of the building.

"What happened?" she asked as soon as they were outside.

"Not much," he said grimly. "They did give me access to the files, but basically told me to stay out of it."

They climbed into his car and started back to the hotel.

Marli tried to sort out her confused thoughts. Trey was on a leave of absence. She didn't know the details of what had happened with his job, although an intense curiosity itched inside her, but it must have been bad. She knew he wanted to be involved in the case. Hell, he *was* involved now, whether he wanted to be or not, thanks to her. On the other hand, she worried for his safety as much as for her own.

Oh, jeez. She didn't even know this guy. So he'd saved her life. That didn't mean she had to worship the ground he walked on or fall on a sword for him.

But she was starting to feel like she would. He was an amazing man. Strong, sure, good. She understood these things deep inside her with an instinctive knowledge.

"Why did you get suspended, Trey?" When she wanted to know something, she asked. She didn't really expect him to answer.

"I'd rather not talk about that," he said evenly, concentrating on the busy freeway.

She nodded.

"I had a look at the report you gave the police about Krista."

Her heart sank. There was a lot of stuff in there she'd rather he didn't know.

"Did you tell them everything? Every little detail?"

She nodded. "Well, if you saw the report I'm sure you know I…I drank a lot of tequila that night. Some of the evening is a little fuzzy." She bent her head. "I think I told them everything, though."

"Okay. If you remember anything at all about Barnes, tell me. Okay?"

"Of course." She looked up at his strong profile as he stared out the windshield. "Are we going back to the hotel?"

"Yeah." He wasn't very talkative right now, so she lapsed into silence as well, quiet until they were back in his room.

He threw himself down into one of the chairs in the corner.

Marli lowered herself onto the bed, kicking off her flip-flops. She eyed him. He looked so serious and intent. And so cute.

Watching him talk to those other feds had made her hot. How pathetic was that? Just the sight of Trey talking, albeit in a very professional and sober way, communicating on the same level with those other guys, using terminology and acronyms she didn't understand, made her look at him with respect and—damn it—lust.

She looked at him like that now. She wanted to touch him, to smooth his furrowed brow, press away the crease between his eyebrows, coax his straight, firm mouth into a smile. She sat on her hands to keep from getting up and doing that.

"So, what now?" she asked.

He looked at her.

"We're going back to Cactus Jack's."

CHAPTER 9

She stared at him blankly. "We are?"

He nodded. "I hate to involve you like that, but it's the only thing I can think of."

"Okay."

He gave her a look. "You aren't going to argue with me?"

"Why would I do that?"

"Because every time I try to tell you what to do, you give me grief."

She laughed. "Yeah, well, you *are* bossy. But I was probably going to go there anyway."

His mouth twisted wryly. "I should've known that." He sighed. Damn it, he didn't want her back in that bar, but they had to do something.

"So why the change of heart on your part?" She stood and moved toward him. *Oh, no.* She needed to stay away from him. Far, far away where he couldn't get his hands on her sexy body. He pushed the chair back until it bumped the wall.

She stood before him, not close, but within touching distance if he reached out. That strip of smooth bare skin around her middle kept drawing his eyes. He forced himself to look up at her face.

Mistake. The heat in her eyes was undeniable. Hot desire jolted through him and he almost groaned aloud.

He sucked in a big breath and forced himself to focus. "He was there, Marli. Probably every night. He followed you home from there. Tried to break into your house. The next night, he followed you into the parking garage. He's been there watching you."

He watched her eyes move as she processed what he was saying.

"But I've been looking for him," she said. "Every night. I never saw him."

"Remember, he's changed his appearance by now. Somehow. I think he cut off his hair and dyed it. Darker. That's what the guy in the parking garage looked like."

She nodded thoughtfully. Her hands were trembling, almost imperceptibly.

Damn. He had to touch her. He reached out for her cold hands, holding them between both of his much bigger ones. He pulled her a little closer.

"He's been there the whole time," he repeated. "And so have you. So maybe he'll be there again. Only this time, I'll be there, too, watching for him." He got up and went over to his suitcase, and, from beneath a pile of clothes, he pulled out his Glock.

Marli let out a little gasp.

"Sorry, sweetheart," he said, "but I think we need this tonight."

She nodded again, her sparkly green and gold eyes huge in her face. He came back to her, leaving the gun on the dresser. He set his hands on her waist and looked directly into her eyes. "Can you handle this?"

She just stared back at him for a long moment, then gave a short, jerky nod. "I have to," she said firmly. "For Krista."

He nodded, too. Without conscious thought, he drew her closer to him, absorbing the heat of her. That spicy mixture of vanilla, cinnamon and musk from the shampoo and conditioner she'd used earlier surrounded him. His fingers slipped under the hem of her tank top to find warm, bare skin.

"You're so strong," he said softly, fingers moving over her skin. She shivered at his touch.

"No, I'm not. I'm terrified. But I'm even more terrified of not getting that bastard. He…raped and killed my friend, set her on…f-fire." Her voice choked with emotion. She met his eyes. "I'll do whatever I have to do."

"Why?" he murmured, fingers sliding higher, under her top. "Why are you so invested in this? Why can't you just let the police deal with it?"

"They're *not* dealing with it!" She swayed closer to him, her eyes glazing over with his caresses. "Look what's been happening. He's trying to kill *me* now."

Trey didn't want to agree with her, but damn it, he was afraid she was right. He stroked up her back, then down, in long, slow brushes of his fingertips. God, she was soft. And warm. "But before you met me, you were determined to do this, even though your plan was insanely dangerous and stupid."

"Oh, thank you very much."

Her breasts touched his chest. Her nipples were hard. He could feel them right through her lace bra and the thin top, and he nearly panted with need.

"It wasn't that dangerous. If I saw him in the bar, what would he do to me? I don't think he'd hurt me in front of hundreds of people."

"Maybe not. But he'd definitely get away before you could even call the police, let alone have them show up there."

"Yeah. Probably. Okay, so I wasn't thinking straight." She sighed and ducked her head. "If you read the report, then you know what happened that night."

"Why don't you tell me?" He bent his head, wanting to taste her. He touched his lips to the side of her neck, where her skin was thin, fragile, silky. He breathed in the scent of her and his body twitched hard.

Her head fell back and her eyes closed. "Trey."

"Right here."

"How can you expect me to talk when you're doing that to me?"

He kissed her neck again and sucked a little bit, tasting her. She was so sweet. Her hands came up to his shoulders and held on. He loved how she responded to his touch. She clearly wanted him as much as he wanted her. No reason to hesitate or wonder if she'd reject him. Even so, his heart pounded hard in his chest; his breath hitched.

He took her mouth then, one hand sliding into her hair—that hair!—wrapping the long curls around his fingers and tugging her head to the right place. He tilted his head and kissed her.

It was like an explosion went off deep inside him, and he dimly thought she felt the same thing as she gasped into his mouth. He opened his mouth over hers, touched her lips with his tongue, tasting her, teasing her. Then he plunged his tongue in a deep, devouring kiss, his hand tightening in her hair, the other arm sweeping her up against him hard.

He pressed her to him, breasts flattened against his chest as he ate at her mouth hungrily. And she kissed him back, just as eager, her small tongue licking his. Her hands clutched his shoulders as she struggled to get closer, practically climbing onto him with her excitement.

He was so rock-hard he hurt. A red-hot rush of desire surged through him, setting him on fire for her. He took her mouth again and again, crushing her soft mouth in deep, demanding kisses that still weren't enough. Her mouth was sweet, warm and delicious.

He picked her up by her ass, pulling her against his raging hard-on, and she was soft and oh, so hot there. She wrapped those long legs around him, and now he did groan, a rough sound that came from deep within him.

They fell together onto the bed, rolling, legs twined around each other, his erection bumping her softness, and she pressed her mound back against him eagerly, desperately, grinding. Their mouths connected again, feverish, seeking, devouring. Then, panting and wide-eyed, she drew back to look at him. A scorching haze enveloped them, and he took a huge, shuddering breath.

"Marli." He pulled her head back down to him to take her mouth again. He rolled her over so he pinned her to the mattress, thrusting his hands into her hair to hold her head there for his kisses. She sucked his lip into her mouth, then bit him hard enough to make him gasp, and wicked sensations sizzled down his spine. Her tongue stroked his lip, pushed into his mouth and he sucked on her, almost frantic with a desperate, urgent need to take. Take everything.

He rolled back, taking her with him so now she was on top and she straddled him. He reached for the hem of her tank top and shoved it up. The low-cut lacy cups of her bra revealed the curves of her breasts sweetly spilling out. There was that mole. He pressed his mouth to it, traced his tongue over it, then turned his face into the curve of one breast and inhaled, her scent intoxicating him, making his head whirl.

He grabbed the tank top and yanked it over her head, tossed it aside, while she reached behind her back and undid the bra. It, too, disappeared, and then she was sitting astride him, her soft, hot pussy pressed to his cock, naked from the hips up. God, she was beautiful.

With dazed wonder, he moved his hands over her flat belly, up to feel the weight of her full breasts. Desire surged through him and his hips lifted, thrusting his hard-on into her softness. Her eyes closed, her face tight with raw need, and she quivered beneath his touch.

She opened her eyes, appearing bemused herself, and reached for the buttons of his shirt. She undid the top one, then the next, then impatiently slid her hands inside to feel his chest. He gasped at the touch of her fingers on his chest, his nipples.

He pulled her down and rolled again, twining his legs with hers, trapping her against him, heat to heat, kissing her again, wrapping his arms around her in a crushing embrace.

"Trey," she gasped, wrenching her mouth away from his, "stop. Please."

He could barely hear her over the roaring in his ears. Somehow, he managed to regain a fragment of control and gulped in a breath. "What?" he gasped. "What's wrong?"

She rolled away from him and lay on the edge of the bed, her back to him. As he tried to focus his blurry vision, he pressed a hand to his fly, his cock throbbing painfully behind it.

She was so slender he could see every vertebra curving from her smooth neck down to the swell of her bottom in those soft yoga pants. He watched her ribs rise and fall quickly with her agitated breathing.

"What is it, Marli?" he asked, straining to keep his voice gentle. But Christ, he was so turned on he could barely see straight.

"I can't do this."

He was silent. She'd been doing just fine a minute ago. More than fine. *Ho, boy.* He took a deep breath and blew it out.

"I'm sorry," she muttered into the pillow. "I just can't."

Communicating with women wasn't one of his strengths…witness his train wreck of a marriage. Marli wasn't his wife…hell, she wasn't *anything* to him, except…important. So important. He wanted to do this right.

He rolled onto his back and stared at the ceiling, trying in vain to control the blood rushing to his dick and the furious pounding of his heart.

"Please, tell me why," he whispered. "Talk to me, sweetheart."

She was silent, but he waited, calling on every ounce of patience he possessed. Her heard her sniffle, then felt her roll, too. He turned his head and saw she lay beside him, her head on the pillow next to him. He reached up a hand and took her chin, tugging toward him so she faced him. He touched her mouth with his fingertips, then removed his hand. They weren't touching, just lying side by side, looking at each other. Even with eyes shadowed with pain, her mouth pinched, she was so beautiful.

"It's just wrong…to be…enjoying myself like this. At a time like this. Krista's dead," she said baldly. "I should not be doing this."

"Oh, Marli." He'd talked to victims' families so many times and he knew what she was talking about. "It's okay, honey. Life goes on." He reached out and touched her cheek with gentle fingertips.

Slowly, she lifted her hand and grabbed hold of his, pressing it to her face. "But it feels so wrong," she cried softly. "To go on with *my* life, when *hers* is over."

"I know."

She gazed back at him. Then she closed her eyes. "You were asking me earlier why I was so determined to find her killer."

"Yeah." He waited.

Eyes still closed, still gripping his hand and holding it to her cheek, she started to talk. "The night Krista was murdered, she and I had a big argument." She stopped and squeezed her eyes closed tighter.

Trey waited.

"She met…Rob…Sheldon…whoever. He was a smooth talker, and she really liked him. Then I sat down, and he started flirting with me a bit." She took a breath and opened her eyes. "I wasn't flirting with him," she said earnestly, eyes pleading with him to believe her. "I just…talk…and stuff comes out. I would never try to take a guy away from Krista. But she was mad. We'd both had a lot to drink. My fault again," she said a little bitterly. "I didn't want to be at a stupid country bar, so I was ordering tequila shots for everyone. Then Krista was telling me that I'm always attracting guys' attention, always flirting with them. She told me to back off. I was so pissed off." She paused, gripped his hand even tighter. "I don't *do* that."

"I know, sweetheart." He did. He'd seen it happen. She just said things, but she was so sexy and appealing it came across as not so innocent. He'd seen her suddenly become aware of how her words sounded and close up because of it.

"Thank you," she whispered. "But Krista thought I did. I couldn't believe it. We were best friends since high school. Like sisters. We're both different—she was much quieter and more reserved than I am—but I loved her. I wouldn't do anything to hurt her. I never realized all those years that she was thinking stuff like that about me. It hurt me."

"Yeah."

"And the worst thing is, when she went to leave with Sheldon, I was hurt and mad, and I practically dared her to do it. Rachel started to try to tell her she shouldn't be leaving with a stranger, and I just…let her." Her eyes closed again and a tear squeezed out and rolled down her smooth cheek.

"It's all my fault she's dead," she whispered. "And I can't bear it. I can't bear the thought that she's gone, and that she died hating me. And now she's gone, and I can never tell her how sorry I am."

Trey reached for her instinctively, pulling her into his arms. She buried her face into his neck, shaking, and one of her hands fisted in his shirt. *Ah, shit.* Yeah, he'd read the report, but none of Marli's tortured feelings had come out of that. *Christ.* He ran his hand down her back, and even though she was half-naked in his arms, he just wanted to hold her and comfort her.

"Hey," he said, after a while, "you can't torture yourself like this." Although he knew only too well the feeling.

She sniffled. "Easy to say," she said. "I asked you this once before…do you follow your own advice?"

He smiled against her hair. "You know I don't. But don't do as I do. Do as I say."

"I don't take orders from you, Special Agent Nicholson."

He kissed her hair. "You told me once that you were jealous of Krista's hair."

"Yeah." She pulled back and looked up at him, confused. "So?"

"Does that mean you didn't love her?"

"Of course not. I did love her."

"So Krista could be jealous of your…outgoing personality, but that doesn't mean she didn't love you, Marli."

She stared at him, and another fat tear rolled from her eye. "You're right," she whispered, looking at him in wonder. "God, you're right, Trey."

He hugged her closer. "I know that doesn't help with all the big questions, like why it happened. I know you feel guilty about not stopping her. Because you're a good person. But what happened to her is *not* your fault, Marli. No way, no how."

She curled into him, hanging onto him.

He'd never felt closer to anyone than he did to her at that moment. Not just physically, although she was as close as they could get without him being inside her. But emotionally, he connected with her, knew what she was feeling, understood where it was coming from. God, he'd never even felt like this with Lisa, sad to say.

His hands moved over her back soothingly, stroking her soft skin with the intent to comfort, not arouse. They lay like that, curled together, for long, quiet moments, tenderness and some indefinable emotion making something in his chest expand and soften.

CHAPTER 10

Well, she'd killed that mood.

Marli nuzzled her face into Trey's neck. God, he smelled good. She sniffed at him, then pressed her mouth to his skin, a soft, open-mouthed kiss. Emotions rose and fell inside her like lava in a lava lamp. It was such a relief to have finally told someone how she felt. Somehow, it shrunk the guilt and anguish down to size. Didn't get rid of them…and that was okay. But now, maybe she could handle it.

Trey was so amazing. How had he known? She supposed in his work he'd dealt with so much grief and sorrow he knew what people were going through. The fact that he understood her when she barely understood herself, though, touched something deep inside her. Made her soften, warm to him more than she already had. Jesus, next thing she knew she'd be thinking she was falling in love with him. Her hero.

She had to remember Trey was a cop, doing a job, passing through town, a man with shadows and secrets of his own that dogged him. Definitely not someone to fall in love with.

Slowly, she pulled out of his arms and again rolled to the edge of the bed, reaching down to the floor for her tank top. She slipped it over her head so she was semi-covered, although a quick glance down at her chest saw her beaded nipples were clearly on display through the thin white cotton.

She swallowed words that would tell him about the strange, soft emotions she was feeling for him. "I could use some food," she said instead.

He lifted his wrist so he could see his watch. “Yeah,” he said. “It’s seven o’clock. By the time we get something to eat, it’ll be time to go.”

She nodded, her tummy tightening. But tonight Trey would be with her. Really with her. Looking out for her.

She stood and went to find clothes to change into. She pulled her jeans out of her bag and slipped out of the loose yoga pants. *Hmmm...* She’d change her underwear. A quick glance behind her told her that, yes, Trey was watching her, with those intense eyes. She paused, then put her thumbs into the elastic band of the panties and shimmied out of them, her back to him. She felt his eyes burning into her like a brand as she searched for clean panties. She’d never felt so self-conscious in her life. She, who never felt self-conscious. She knew he was watching and wanted him so much to like what he saw.

She found the pink thong she’d tossed in, and stepped into it, adjusting the thin straps on her hips. Then she reached for the hem of the tank top and pulled it over her head, dropping it into the duffle bag. She tugged out a pink cotton T-shirt bra. Not her sexiest underwear, but that’s not what she’d been thinking about when she’d fled her house last night. *This morning. Whatever.* She fastened the bra behind her and then pulled a long, snug navy blue T-shirt on. She ran her fingers through her hair and then glanced again at Trey before going into the bathroom.

He was still watching her and made no attempt to look away, all smoldering, dark intensity, lounging there on the bed with one knee bent, his shirt untucked and half unbuttoned. She turned so fast to go into the washroom that she ran smack into the wall.

“Ow!” *God, how embarrassing.* She fled into the bathroom and closed the door behind her with a sharp click, setting her hands on the counter, leaning forward. Her entire body burned. Things were getting way too intense.

She splashed cold water on her face, combed through her wildly tangled curls, touched up her makeup.

When she came out, Trey was just zipping up the fly on his jeans. He’d left the white shirt on, loose over the low-slung jeans, but he’d done up one more button over his chest. He ran his hands through his own mussed hair.

She met his eyes, and the air grew charged and hot around them. His pupils shot wide, making his eyes even darker.

“Trey.”

“Mmm.”

"I do want you."

No sense beating around the bush. When she had something to say, she said it.

His lips quirked. "Yeah?"

She nodded. "I don't know what's going to happen tonight. So I just wanted you to know that."

"Christ, Marli, nothing's going to happen tonight. And now I have to sit in that bar all night with a hard-on, just waiting to get you back here so I can have you."

Her knees went so soft she thought she might fall. That aching need between her legs was back. Her fresh panties were damp already.

"Me, too." Her eyes made him promises he seemed to understand and reciprocate.

"Let's go."

They ate in the restaurant in the inn, a family-type place full of parents and their kids on holidays. Marli picked at a club sandwich and fries, while Trey devoured another huge meal, a steak sandwich, fries and a big piece of apple pie with ice cream.

When they finished, they looked at each other.

"Showtime," Trey said quietly. He paid the bill and they went out to his car in the dusky parking lot.

* * *

Trey drove around and around until he found a spot on the street not far from Marli's car. When they left, he wanted to be close to her. He parked and they started toward Cactus Jack's. He stopped her on the sidewalk around the corner from the bar.

"We can't go in together," he said quietly. "We want it to look like you're there alone again. Just go sit at the bar. Try to find two chairs so I can join you."

She looked up at him with wide eyes. Christ, he hated sending her in there alone after everything that had happened. "I'll be right behind you," he said roughly. "Even if I don't sit down right away. Okay?"

She nodded.

"Remember. Don't look at just the guys with blond hair. You have to look at everyone."

"Yes."

He stared at her for a long moment, eyes moving over her face, then bent and kissed her hard on the mouth. Then he turned her by the shoulders and gave her a little push. With a glance over her shoulder, she went around the corner and entered the bar. He watched her go in and waited for the longest moments of his life. Then he, too, strolled casually in.

He spotted her at the bar with his peripheral vision. *Good girl.* Empty chair beside her, at the end where he liked.

Instead of heading directly to the bar, he pushed through the crowd toward the two pool tables at the back. He stood and watched people play, smiling as if he were enjoying the game, but eyeballing everyone around. Hands in his jeans pockets, he leaned against a rough-hewn post and turned to survey the bar.

The music twanged loudly, people danced with abandon and a burst of laughter came from a nearby table where two girls shrieked with hilarity over something. He smiled. Casually, he strolled the length of the bar, then said to Marli, "Anyone sitting here?"

She shook her head and turned away from him to watch the dance floor. The bartender slid a glass of Coke across the bar to her and she gave him a quick smile of thanks.

"I'll have a Surf Coast Pale Ale," he said, before the bartender disappeared with a scowl.

He shrugged and looked at Marli, and she met his eyes and gave him a faint smile.

"So what's new?" he asked.

"Nothing."

They both searched the room. "We might have to dance," he said. "Otherwise, it's too dark to see everyone over there."

She nodded. "If we must."

He grinned. His beer arrived and he drank thirstily. *One. Just one.* No way was he screwing up again when Marli's life was on the line.

"Did you know that if you dance on the bar here you win a free thong?" she asked conversationally.

He choked on his beer and she smacked him on the back, laughing.

"Really."

"Don't worry. I won't do it tonight," she assured him. "I've already got my thong."

He groaned.

"I did that the night Krista was killed," she continued, a bit sadly. "That was another thing that made her mad. She thought I was trying to attract Rob's attention."

"God, I am so out of my league with you."

She laughed.

They danced to Tim McGraw singing "When The Stars Go Blue," dragging their eyes away from each other's faces to search the dance floor for anyone who might be Sheldon Barnes. After, they sipped their drinks and talked at the bar.

"Tell me about your family," he asked her.

"I have a very normal, boring family. My dad is a doctor and my mom is an interior designer. She wanted to be an artist, but decided a career as a designer was more practical. I have two brothers, both younger than me. Brett is twenty-six and Jason is twenty-three. They were both extremely annoying pests when we were little, but now they're okay." She grinned. "Brett is almost finished medical school. Jason works for IBM."

"Very solid upper middle class."

"Absolutely. I'm very lucky. We have a lot of fun when we get together." She peered at him. "Why won't you tell me about your family?"

He looked at the beer glass with the inch of warm beer he was nursing. "We're kind of estranged," he said finally. "My parents and my sister felt sorry for me after what happened, and I just couldn't handle their pity. So I just stay away from them. For now."

"But someday you'll reconcile with them. Right?"

He shrugged. "I guess so."

"Family's important."

"Hey, I know it," he said. "Especially now, I know it. But shit happens."

"Are you waiting for one of them to make the first move?" Her voice was warm with curiosity.

He thought about that. Did he want his mom or his sister to hunt him down, force him to see them? Not really. "No."

"Then *you're* going to make the first move."

He glared at her. "You don't know what you're talking about."

He saw the hurt in her eyes the minute the words left his lips and regretted it. "I'm sorry," he apologized immediately. "I didn't mean to snap at you."

"I don't know what I'm talking about because you won't tell me," she snapped back at him. "You're too *macho* to talk about your feelings, to tell me what happened to split your family up."

"I'm not macho," he protested. "I'm just not ready to talk about it."

"You made me talk about my issues," she reminded him,

challenging him.

"I know." Now he felt bad. But not bad enough to spill his guts and tell Marli what a screw-up he was. In his work and his personal life. And how he'd cost her best friend her life. "If I was going to talk to anyone, I'd talk to you," he said softly, repeating her words to him.

A reluctant smile played about her mouth.

"I guess I'll take that." She shook her head at him. "For now. At least tell me…both your parents are still living?"

"Yes."

"And you have a sister."

"Yes."

"That's it?"

He paused. "And…and a brother."

"You're the oldest, aren't you?"

He looked at her warily. "How'd you know that?"

"'Cause you're so bossy," she said sweetly.

"You're the oldest, too," he pointed out.

She grinned. "I know." She swirled the ice in her glass. "So what do they all do?"

"My dad's a cop. Surprise, surprise. Mom stayed at home. She worked part-time from home doing the books for some small businesses. My sister is now a lawyer."

"And…your brother?"

Is an asshole, he thought. Pain shot through him, but it wasn't like it used to be. That unbearable, agonizing feeling of betrayal was, amazingly, fading. "He's a computer hardware expert. He has his own business and goes around defragging people's hard drives or something."

She nodded thoughtfully. "Why're you mad at him?"

He shot her a sharp look. "What makes you think I'm mad at him?"

"Intuition. Gut instinct. The look on your face when you talk about him."

"How about those Padres?" he asked and was relieved when she laughed.

By one o'clock, Marli was yawning behind her hand and Trey was frustrated. "I guess we pack it in for tonight," he growled into her ear. "Here's the part I really don't like. We have to leave separately."

He saw her tighten her lips. "That's okay." Determination hardened her voice. She tossed some bills on the bar to pay for her meager bar bill, enough to include a generous tip for the poor bartender who'd brought her two Diet Cokes.

"Go to your car," he instructed her. "Drive home. I'll be right behind you." He looked around the bar. "I'll go first," he muttered. "Stay here for five minutes."

Shit, shit, shit. Again, he hated leaving her there. But there'd been no sign of Barnes, so he'd be better off outside, waiting in his vehicle to watch her leave.

His SUV, unfortunately, was parked four vehicles in front of hers, so he had to watch for her out the back window. He tried to stay low in case anyone else was watching. He looked around. *Damn.* This street hadn't been so dark and deserted earlier in the evening.

He waited impatiently for Marli, heart thumping slow and strong in his chest. Then he saw her. She was walking quickly to her car along the deserted sidewalk.

Son of a bitch. His heart jumped into his throat and he almost choked.

CHAPTER 11

A shadow had emerged from the alley behind the bar, sticking close to the buildings. Trey threw open the door and tried to jump out, twisting awkwardly because he'd been facing backward.

"Marli!" he shouted, reaching for the gun at his back. The shadowy figure stopped, turned toward him, hands raised and outstretched. The bastard had a gun, too.

Trey dove over the hood of his vehicle as a bullet popped, then ripped into the fender. He rose up and took aim, pausing only to ensure Marli was away from his line of sight. He heard Marli scream his name.

"Marli, get down!" he shouted, and squeezed the trigger. It was dark and it was a long shot and…

The guy turned and ran. "Not this time, you sonofabitch," he muttered as he scrambled around the hood of the SUV and ran towards Marli. She leaned on her car, hand on her chest, eyes huge and frightened.

"You okay?" he demanded, skidding to a stop. Adrenaline rushed through his veins.

"I'm okay. Are you okay? Trey, my God…"

"I'm okay…I'm going after him."

"No…"

He was gone, running before she even got the word out. He spared a moment's thought for the fact he was leaving her alone again. The two gunshots didn't even attract any attention from people in the area, which was pretty scary. You'd think people would come running.

Thoughts ran through his mind as he raced along the sidewalk, around the corner and stopped. Gone. Disappeared into thin air. Unless he'd gone back into the bar. *Fuck, no.*

Barnes had a gun. Now he was really dangerous—and in a crowded bar.

Trey debated, his mind a whirling jumble of thoughts. Then he grabbed his cell phone and called 911.

He turned and jogged back to Marli, shivering in her car with the doors locked.

"Attagirl," he murmured when she opened the door for him. She leaped out and into his arms.

"Trey, God, Trey, he shot at you." She ran her hands over his body urgently. "Oh, my God."

"I'm okay," he murmured, pulling her close. He juggled gun and cell phone. "We need to get out of here."

"Yes. Yes."

"My vehicle." He led her up the street. He drove quickly to his hotel, constantly checking to make sure they weren't being followed.

"This is insane," she said, teeth chattering again as they went up in the elevator.

"Cops will likely be here soon." He let her into the room. Once the door closed behind them, he took her in his arms again and held her tightly. "Jesus, Marli, I thought I was having a heart attack. Did you know he was behind you?"

"No." She shook her head quickly. "I heard you yell and the next thing I know he's shooting. God, Trey, I was afraid he killed you."

"He dinged my new car, goddamn it."

She stared at him, then grabbed his face in both hands and kissed him, desperately, urgently. He kissed her back, just as frantically, hands going up and down her back as if to assure himself she was there, unharmed.

* * *

That was it. That was the last time. He wasn't an idiot. They'd really be looking for him now. *Fuck.* He knew they could never catch him, he was way above that, but he also knew when to cut his losses. He was out of here.

Anyway, staying here to punish Marli wasn't really part of his plans. He had bigger things to do.

Why did Mr. Big-and-Tall keep showing up? And why the hell did he have a gun? That wasn't supposed to happen. They'd sat there all night, wasting time, dancing, gazing into each other's eyes. When the guy'd finally left her sitting there alone, excitement rose and adrenaline kicked in. "Last chance, last chance," he'd chanted as he followed her.

Laura was probably looking for him, but who cared. He was done there now. He had a pocketful of money that would keep him going for a while.

He gathered up his meager belongings and left the motel. He checked the money in his pocket. He'd made a fair bit on tips tonight, so he could afford to take a cab. He directed the driver to the Honky Tonk Bar and Grill, just on the outskirts of town.

The place was hopping and he soon spotted just what he wanted. She was young, blonde and alone. Not exactly pretty, nothing like Marli, but she looked kind of sad and lonely.

"Hey, gorgeous," he said with a friendly smile. "Can I buy you a drink?"

* * *

The police and the two FBI special agents they'd met earlier arrived at the hotel to take statements. Again.

"I'm getting so tired of this," Marli said wearily. She looked at Trey. "When is it going to end? I don't know how much more I can take."

"Something's going on with him," Trey said with irritation. "This isn't his usual behavior."

"Why is he doing this to me?"

Trey scowled. "Well, because you're blonde for one thing."

"Why?" she demanded. "Why are all his victims blonde?"

"His mother is blonde," Trey replied. "They have a…difficult relationship. Plus, I think it's because you laughed at him when he told you he was a cowboy."

"Huh?"

He recalled his conversation with Sheldon's brother and told Marli and the other FBI agents about it.

"I went to see his brother Peter when I was investigating Kathy Richards' murder."

Special Agent Burrows nodded. "It's in the file."

Trey continued, for Marli's benefit. "Peter's blonde and good-looking like Sheldon, except he looks rough, like he's been through hell. Life of crime, like Sheldon. Apparently, Sheldon was a hyper kid. Peter thought he probably had ADD or ADHD, said he was always acting out, running around, bouncing off the walls."

* * *

Brawley, California
Seven months earlier

"Drove the rest of your family crazy?" Trey asked Peter.

"Oh, yeah. Especially my mama. She gets pretty stressed herself. One time, she locked him in the closet in his bedroom just to keep him quiet and out of her way. She left him there for two days. Another time she almost drowned him, she was so pissed because he was fooling around in the tub and splashing water all over the floor. She held his head under water, and he was choking so much, I thought he was gonna die."

Trey's gut clenched, listening to the stories of emotional and physical abuse.

"One time when he was bigger, and she could hardly hold him down, she tied him up. Tied his wrists to the bed. His wrists were bleeding, he tried so hard to get away.

"Sheldon was always gettin' into trouble at school," Peter continued. "That's why he dropped out so early. Started drinkin' and doin' drugs when he was only, like, eleven or twelve. But it was never his fault. Mama would go to school and try to find out who was giving him a hard time."

"If he was in trouble all the time, it must have been at least partly his fault."

Peter laughed shortly. "It was *always* his fault," he said. "He never could take responsibility, and Mama was just like that, too. Someone else was getting her little boy in trouble."

"Tell me about his wife."

"Teresa," Peter replied. "They sure weren't married long. He knocked her up when she was still in high school, but she left before the baby was even born. Actually, I heard she had twins, boys. Sheldon was beatin' on her and that's why she took off. I don't even know where she lives now, and she probably likes it that way."

Trey said nothing.

"Sheldon was drivin' a cab when they got married, but he'd always wanted to be a cowboy. Mama used to laugh at him when he said that, and make fun of him, call him "cowboy" in that nasty tone she had, and it sure made him mad. So then he took off one day and sure enough, he got a job at some ranch, cleaning stables or something, I dunno. Anyway, we didn't see him for a long time after that. Every once in a while he'd come home lookin' for money, and we thought he was probably in some kind of trouble."

* * *

Trey paused and looked at Marli's pale, tense face. "Wanda Barnes apparently thought bullying her children was the way to control their behavior, and Sheldon was too impulsive to control his anger. Women with blonde hair—like Wanda's—apparently trigger his anger—and suffer for what he probably wanted to do to his mother when he was a boy."

"Oh, God," Marli said, pulling her own hair. "I had no idea."

"Of course not. Don't start beating yourself up about that, too. You had no idea he was nuts."

Special Agent Burrows glanced at him. "What do you think his next move is?"

"Wish I had a hot clue," Trey said, rubbing his face. "But we're not going back to that bar."

"You shouldn't have done that tonight," Burrows said sharply. "You should know better than to endanger the life of a civilian."

Trey nodded regretfully.

"What are you talking about?" Marli demanded. "He didn't endanger me; he saved me. I was the one who planned to go there, just like I've been going there every night this week. Trey just came to look after me."

Trey looked at her wordlessly, keeping his face expressionless. Something flickered in her eyes, passing between them.

Burrows looked at Trey. "That true?"

Trey still looked at Marli. "She says it, it must be true."

Burrows scowled.

When they'd gone, Trey gave Marli a measured look. "I don't like lying."

"I know." She gave him a small smile. "But I wasn't really lying."

He shook his head, helplessly fascinated and annoyed by her. "You wouldn't lie to *me*, would you?" He walked toward her, deliberately, intently. Chasing criminals gave him an adrenaline rush that somehow always turned into raw sexual need. His body still pulsed from the scene outside the bar.

She watched him with a heated gaze. "I would never lie to you, Trey."

"Remember what you said earlier?" He stood in front of her.

"Oh, yeah."

"Not a lie?"

"Nope."

"Good."

CHAPTER 12

Marli shivered with excitement as she watched Trey approach her, now alone in the hotel room. She was burning for him, wet and desperate, aching with emptiness, pulsing with need. Her nipples hardened almost painfully, her breasts tight and full. She wanted to finish what they'd started earlier.

His eyes were so hot she melted. Waves of intensity shimmered off him, almost frightening her.

He stopped in front of her, their bodies as close as they could be without touching. Heat radiated off him, every muscle and tendon in his body taut. A pulse throbbed in his tight jaw.

She put a hand up to that jaw, touched him softly, let her fingers trail over the strong jawbone and down his neck, and his eyes darkened even more. He shuddered and stared at her mouth. Her lips parted.

"I was so scared for you tonight," she whispered. She touched his face again, stroked one thick, dark eyebrow, touched a high cheekbone. With the back of her hand, she rubbed her knuckles across his lean cheek, rough with dark stubble, trailed her thumb across his bottom lip. Strong white teeth nipped the pad of that thumb and she smiled, letting him lick her thumb. Then she rubbed her wet thumb across his lip again.

God, he could've been killed, with that lunatic shooting at him, and then Trey'd chased after him. Her legs went mushy.

"*You* were scared," he muttered. "Christ, Marli, I've been a cop for nearly eight years. I've never lost my mind like that. If he'd shot you…" He groaned, a raw, agonized sound, and he swept her into his arms and kissed her over and over.

Her mouth opened for him, her tongue met his, twined with his in a hot, wet kiss that went on and on and on. Her body dissolved as Trey snugged her closer, his big hands on her hips, pressing her against his erection.

She pushed into him, arching in his possessive hold. A moan tore from her throat. "God, I need you." Exquisite heat throbbed between her legs and in her nipples. Tiny needles of hot sensation prickled her skin, every nerve ending jumping, everything inside her pulling up.

He let out a ragged groan in response, hands cupping her butt, pulling her harder against him. His big thigh slid between her legs, and she climbed him, ground her pelvis against him, gasping as she strained closer. Then, mindlessly, breathlessly, she came. "Ohhhh." Her body spasmed against his, quivery sensation rippling from her core through her body. Trey held her while she climaxed, riding his thigh, pleasure cascading over her, then her body sank into him as it softened.

"Jesus, Marli, what was that?"

She moaned, her face tucked against his chest. She couldn't believe that had just happened. "God, Trey, don't you know?"

He gave a soft laugh. "Yeah, I know. I just can't believe it. You are so hot."

"I can't help it. You make me hot."

She was draped over him like a wet hotel towel. He still vibrated with tightly controlled need. "I'm sorry." She drew back to look in his face. "I should've waited for you."

"Hell, no," he said roughly. "It's not like you only get one chance to come. I'm gonna make you come again. And again, until you're out of your mind."

A sharp jolt of heat shot through her womb at his words. He worked her long T-shirt up over her thighs and hips, then all the way over her head.

"No, wait." Her hands tugged his away from the button of her jeans. "I want *you* naked." She started to unbutton his shirt.

"Oh, yeah. I want me naked, too. With you naked. In that bed. Like, yesterday."

She tried to get her shaking fingers to work on the small buttons. Then she pushed the sides of his shirt apart. "I love your chest," she murmured, smoothing her hands across his muscles.

"I like yours, too."

She looked up at him, smiling. Their gazes caught and held. Humor and lust combined in a potent bond that drew them together, connected them.

"Pants off," she said suddenly. "Now." She fumbled with the button of his jeans, and he brushed her hands aside to unzip himself on one neat motion, shoving the jeans easily down over his hips. She bent down to take them all the way off, dragging them away as he stepped out of them, taking his socks with them.

"Yours, too." Hers were a little more effort, fitting snugly as they did, and she wriggled her hips to help him get them off. "God," he breathed the word. "I love how you do that."

Now they stood in their underwear, face to face. Her hands rested on his chest, his on her waist, and they stared at each other.

"Oh, Trey," she whispered and went onto her toes to kiss him, winding her arms around his neck, pressing skin to hot skin. She couldn't believe they were finally doing this, and for this time, even though it was incredibly, decadently pleasurable, it felt right. This was now. What she was doing with Trey had nothing to do with Krista. She gently pushed Krista away into the back of her memory—not forever, just for now—and deepened the kiss, slanting her mouth across his, losing herself in the sensual pleasure of Trey's embrace.

Trey wrapped his arms around her and tumbled her onto the bed, coming down beside her, his body big, heavy and hot. She cried out with pleasure as he cupped one breast, then kissed the other, closing his lips over her budded nipple and sucking. His fingers plucked at the other nipple, and all sensation in her body centered on those two tight little points as he sucked, licked and pulled.

She rolled her head on the bed in ecstasy. She whimpered and fisted her hands in his hair. But his hair was almost too short to get a good grip on, and she raked her nails over his scalp, wringing a gasp from him. He used his teeth on her nipples, making her writhe with an almost unbearable pleasure.

Her hips lifted off the bed, seeking something to fill that empty, aching void, wanting Trey inside her. Her hands moved over his back to his tight butt, to the soft cotton underwear. Slipping around front, she filled her hand with his penis, thick and long. She moaned. Fingers digging, she managed to find the elastic band of the briefs and tug them down over his hips, freeing his hard shaft. He lay on his side, his erection brushing her hip, and she closed her hand around him, yearning to feel him, hot and velvety.

Her thumb brushed over the tip, spreading the warm wetness she found there, making him shudder and groan and twitch in her hand. "I want you inside me."

"Hold on." He rolled away from her, and she whimpered in disappointment.

"What…where are you going?"

He rolled off the bed and strode to the bathroom, returning with a handful of condoms that he tossed onto the bed. She rose up on her elbows, eyed the condoms, then looked at him with a choked laugh.

"Wow," she said. "I'm impressed. Or maybe afraid."

He grinned back at her, waggling his eyebrows, dropping onto the bed beside her and rolling her under him. He snagged one of the condoms and ripped it open.

"Let me, let me," she begged, struggling to sit up. "I've always wanted to do this." Pulse leaping, excitement surging in her, she fumbled a bit, getting it in place.

"Um…inside out, honey," he told her.

She turned it over, started trying to roll it onto him, her fingers groping and slipping. Biting her lip, she glanced up at him and saw his eyes closed as if in pain, jaw clenched.

"Um…I'm not doing very well, am I?"

His hands closed over hers, his eyes shut, stilling her touch. Taking slow, deep breaths, he waited. Finally, he opened his eyes, smiled into hers and brushed her hands away. He pinched the tip and rolled the condom down easily onto his thick shaft.

She admired him, the shape of him, the size of him, the sexy way he touched himself to put the condom on. The aching glow inside her burned even hotter. "Sorry," she whispered. "This isn't the first time I've ever done that, although you might think so."

"Marli."

"Mmm?."

"Shut up and kiss me."

"Oh. You betcha." She stretched herself over him, reaching for his mouth, his hands on her waist lifting and helping her, settling her over him. He pushed her legs apart, his penis nudging at her insistently.

"Yes, yes." She hissed as the big head of his penis thrust at her. She opened her legs wider, lifted over him, then used her fingers to part her labia. *Oh.* She was so wet.

She let her fingers play there with carnal enjoyment, her clit swollen and sensitive. Her lids closed in a slow blink, but when they opened, she saw Trey's eyes darken as he watched her fingers between her legs. His cock twitched.

"Marli."

She smiled at the need roughening his voice.

Trey took hold of himself to guide his penis into her, and oh, he filled her so wonderfully.

She sank onto him, closing her eyes in delight, as she descended on him, lower, lower.

"More, honey," he groaned. "All the way…yes."

She rose up and lowered again, taking all of him, his hard, throbbing length filling her, stretching her.

"God, that's good," she whispered. *So good.* She moved on him, riding him, hands on his chest, crisp hair and hard male nipples against her palms. After long moments of exquisite dragging out and surging in, he grabbed her hands and flipped her over onto her back, managing to do it without leaving her.

"Smooth," she commented, and he choked on a laugh.

Now he was on top of her, driving into her, controlling the pace, sliding in and out with hard, demanding strokes.

"You're so wet, Marli," he murmured. "You feel so good around me, tight and hot and wet."

"Mmmm."

He thrust harder, faster. The world spun away, her consciousness constricting to the incomparable excitement tightening her body. He reached between them and found her clit, slicking up her moisture and rubbing her there. Intense sensation like she'd never experienced shot through her as his penis stroked against a pleasure point inside her and his fingers stroked her clit, the two sensations combining into one intense spiral that twisted and built inside her almost to the point of pain. "Oh. I'm…coming," she managed to say, one heartbeat before she was overcome by wrenching, hard jolts. Lights exploded and sparkled behind her eyes.

"Yeah, honey, that's it. God…" He growled as his body tensed, hard against hers, and he shuddered violently as he came inside her.

Wave after wave of hot pleasure washed over her, leaving her weak and trembling beneath him, even as he pressed into her.

His arms shook and he fell onto her, his big body crushing her, squeezing the air out of her lungs.

"Trey…"

"Sorry," he mumbled. He moved off her, but pulled her tight

against him.

She felt the aftershocks rumble through him for long moments, her own body a quivering mass of excited sensations.

"Holy crap," she murmured, her hand going to his short hair again and ruffling it. A rush of emotion so intense, so hot, so soft, flowed through her and her heart squeezed and swelled up. What had they just done?

CHAPTER 13

"That was too fast," Trey complained into her hair. He'd just climbed back into bed after disposing of the condom.

"Sorry."

"No, no, not you. It was me. I wanted it to last." *Forever.*

"Oh." She lifted her head to look at him. Her eyes sparkled with sexual satisfaction, her lips fuller and darker from his kisses. Her hair was a fiery gold tangle around her head. "Well, I'm not going anywhere."

He smiled. He pushed her away from him, down onto her back and rose up on one elbow to study her. "Good. Because I want to take my time." The rest of their lives might not be enough time for what he wanted to do to her.

His fingertips stroked from her mouth, down to her throat, over her breastbone, between her luscious breasts, over her belly. He stopped at the sparkly little jewels in her bellybutton. "I want to get to know every part of your body. I like this." He gently flicked the barbell.

"Thank you." Her voice was breathy.

"Very sexy." His finger continued, moving lower, stroking through the dark gold curls between her legs. "I want to find all the places that make you crazy," he whispered, looking at her body everywhere he touched. His finger slid lower, into the warm, wet folds. "I want to taste you...here."

He glanced at her face. Her eyes were wide, fascinated, dark with desire, her lips parted.

"I want to lick you and suck on you until you come."

A ragged moan escaped her. She licked her lips.

He turned his attention back to the hand he had buried in her pussy. "Open your legs, sweetheart."

She slowly parted her thighs, giving him better access, and he slicked his fingers up and down. She was wet, so wet and slippery. The sweet musk scent of her rose from his hand as he stroked her. Christ, that was sexy.

He leaned down to kiss her breast, taking one taut nipple into his mouth to suck, run his tongue over, then the other. She tasted like berries, sun-warm and sweet. He kissed the underside of each breast, loving the full curves there, and felt her drag in a sharp breath. He pressed a kiss to her smooth, flat belly, just below her pierced navel, then took the barbell into his mouth and gently tugged on it, eliciting another gasp. He smiled against her flesh.

He shifted his body down the bed to press kisses on each hipbone, then the tender flesh just below, flicking his tongue out to give her little licks on that sensitive place. Her legs twitched restlessly on the bed. "Do you like that?" he murmured.

"I...love...it."

He pulled one thigh toward him, then pushed the other away to open her even more. "Yeah," he said with satisfaction. "I want to see you, too. See how pretty you are." He studied her intimately, admiringly, while his fingers stroked, spreading her slick moisture over her labia, finding her swollen clitoris. When he brushed it, her whole body jerked and quivered. "Oh, yeah." Then he pushed his middle finger inside her, as far as he could, and her hips arched into his hand. He added another finger, her body making soft, wet, sucking noises around his fingers as he thrust in and out.

With excruciating pleasure, he watched as pale, thick fluid oozed out of her around his fingers. His cock grew so hard he hurt, watching how aroused she was. The fluid trickled down, between the cheeks of her ass and, with fascination, he watched it drip onto the bed. He'd never seen a woman so outrageously aroused and it turned him on to the point of pain.

He had to taste her, now, and he leaned forward and lapped up her cream, inhaling deeply, filling himself with her sweet, spicy scent. She shuddered at his touch, her hands going to his hair.

"That feels so good, Trey." She groaned. "God, I want more."

"Mmm." He buried his face between her legs, keeping his fingers inside her, thrusting and licking. His tongue slid up one side, down the other, then up over her clit, making her twitch hard again. She tasted so sweet, and sensation sizzled up his spine. He took her in his mouth and sucked, tongued her again and sucked, then with supreme care, he used his teeth to hold her little clit while he rubbed his tongue over it.

She came then, hard, pressing up into his mouth, crying out. She kept tugging ineffectually at his short hair, but gave up and just held his head against her pussy. He smiled against her, absorbing her enthusiastic and male ego boosting response. When he felt her quaking body grow still, he lifted his mouth from her, looked up her body, met her glazed eyes. She stared back at him, her breasts rising and falling rapidly, and he loved he'd done that to her. His massively engorged dick throbbed with the need to come.

His own heart was racing and he fought the impulse to bury himself in her, but her inner muscles were still contracting around his fingers and it sent him over. He fumbled around over the chaotic bedcovers for another condom, finally finding the packet. He ripped it open and rolled it on. He rose up on his knees and positioned himself between her legs, sliding his elbows beneath her knees and folding her legs back.

The sight of her, spread and open, gleaming and pink, did him in. His patient restraint blew apart and he thrust into her, hard.

She cried out.

Deep, throbbing, biting desire raged through him, an urgent need to have her, take her. He buried himself in her wet heat, lost, out of control, pounding hard into her soft body. With a ferocious groan, his balls tightened and pleasure swept from his cock outward, all the way to his toes, and he convulsed and exploded. His head went back, his body arched and tightened as he poured into her.

"Marli," he gasped, when he had enough air in his lungs, and slumped over her. He released her legs slowly, stroking his hands down her thighs as she stretched them out behind him. "God, Marli."

He slowly withdrew from her body and collapsed beside her, flinging one arm across her. She hugged his arm in a tender gesture that made him feel big, strong and…weak. He squeezed his eyes closed against the emotions rising up inside him.

Then concern for her overrode everything else, and he lifted his head to look at her. "Are you okay?" He reached up with fingers that trembled and touched her cheek. She looked back at him, capturing him with that green and gold gaze, and the warmth and tenderness in her eyes made his breath stick in his throat.

"I'm fine." She reached up to press his hand to her cheek.

He exhaled. "Okay. I was afraid I'd hurt you. I got a little carried away."

"I like that you got carried away." She turned her mouth to his hand and kissed his palm. "I *love* that I do that to you."

Oh.

He flopped back down on the bed and covered his eyes with his free hand. Marli was looking really…loving. God, he hoped she wasn't going to get all emotional just because they'd had sex. His gut tightened.

"Trey?"

He tensed, kept his eyes covered. "Yeah?"

"Life is really precious, isn't it?"

He swallowed. His chest squeezed painfully, and he reached for her, pulled her into his arms, buried his face in her hair. "Yeah."

* * *

Marli turned on her cell phone and punched in the number for her voice mail, biting her lip. "You have sixteen new messages." Her heart sank. She looked at the phone, then flipped it closed and tossed it onto the hotel bed beside her.

She fell back onto the bed and stared at the ceiling. Her life was a mess.

Then why did she feel so incredibly good?

She smiled. Must have been the hot sex and too many screaming orgasms to count last night.

"What?" Trey emerged from the bathroom, toweling his short hair dry, another towel wrapped around his lean hips.

She turned her head to look at him. *Awesome.* She wanted him again. She held out her arms.

He came and stood at the end of the bed, between her legs and looked down at her, his eyes hot and glittery, drops of water sparkling on his broad, brown shoulders.

"Drop the towel," she commanded softly.

With slow movements, he pulled the tucked-in edge of the towel out, drawing it across his body, then let it drop. Marli's mouth went dry as she stared at him. He was a Greek god. Her fingers itched to touch him, run over those sleek, hard muscles. She loved the indentations in his hips, the big, thick muscles of his thighs, and especially she loved…

Whew. He was hard. Again.

"You're beautiful," she told him frankly.

His cheekbones darkened a bit at her open scrutiny. Then he picked up her knees and opened her legs. All she wore was one of his T-shirts, so the movement exposed her intimately to him. She bit her lip. He'd already seen more of her than anyone else in the world, and she might be embarrassed, except the way he looked at her told her he liked what he saw.

"You are gorgeous."

"This isn't going to work."

His lips curved and he gauged the distance between his cock and her vagina. He was tall and the bed was low.

"You're right." He lowered her legs. "Turn over."

She blinked at him, then slowly rolled. The bed gave as he climbed on behind her, then his hands lifted her hips into the air. She pushed up onto her elbows, excitement and desire making her throb and ache.

He held her hips, his knees ruthlessly shoving her legs apart, then he thrust into her from behind. "Oh!" She lowered her forehead to the mattress as he filled her, withdrew, filled her again. He slid in and out, strokes getting faster, harder, his flesh slapping against hers, and it was so incredibly erotic. She pushed her butt back against him to deepen the thrust and heard him growl.

She pushed her hand down under herself, finding her clit.

"Yeah, honey, that's it," he muttered, pumping into her. "Make yourself come."

She moaned as she rubbed herself. Every stroke of his cock inside her made each stroke of her fingers more intense and a fast, hard orgasm shook her, sending her flying into shimmering, shuddering ecstasy.

She was still riding the wave when he tensed and tightened against her, thrust hard once, twice…then withdraw. She whimpered, but then felt liquid warmth on her back and she dimly realized he hadn't used a condom. He held her hips with hard fingers as he spurted onto her.

"God," he gasped. "Sorry, sorry."

She couldn't speak, couldn't breathe. As he pulled away, she stretched out her legs so she lay flat on her stomach and buried her face in her arms. She heard him go into the bathroom, heard water running and then he was wiping off her back with a warm, wet cloth.

Tenderly, carefully he cleaned her, even moving the cloth gently down between her legs.

"I'm sorry," he said again.

She rolled over, arms above her head, one knee bent. "It's okay," she assured him, her heart still thumping madly. "I'm just glad you remembered, 'cause I sure wasn't thinking about that."

He stood there looking down at her, naked and gorgeous, still half-hard and throbbing, his face solemn. "I shouldn't have done that," he said, his voice low and a bit shaky. "It's too big a risk."

"Chill," she told him, a bit puzzled by his intensity. "I'm on the pill. I won't get pregnant and…I won't give you anything."

His eyes widened. "Oh. Okay. Well, I…I… Shit." His throat worked. "I'd better get tested."

CHAPTER 14

Her mouth dropped open. "Explain, please."

Trey had only had sex with one woman in the last six years. He'd been with Lisa six years, married five years, faithful that whole time. He'd felt safe. Until he remembered that, although he'd been faithful, his wife hadn't.

That memory slammed into him like a punch to the gut.

He turned away from Marli and ran his hands though his hair in agony and frustration. "Goddamn it."

She sat up on the bed, pulling the T-shirt down. Waited. "Trey, we just had sex. You need to tell me what that meant."

"I... It's probably okay," he managed to choke out. "God, Marli, I never meant to put you at risk. I was thinking about pregnancy, not about...STDs. I know my own history, but...someone cheated on me. I just realized... God, I am so sorry."

"Oh." The unspoken questions hovered in the air between them.

Travis, you sonofabitch, you'd better have been practicing safe sex or I will kick your ass so hard...

He sighed. He went over to Marli and lifted her up off the bed and into his arms. He looked her straight in the eye. "I promise you I'll get tested as soon as I can, and I'll let you know what the results are. If I've done anything to...I'll never forgive myself."

She nodded, actually amazingly calm considering. "I trust you, Trey," she said. "We'll just make sure we use a condom from now on. But Trey...who cheated on you?"

The soft compassion in her eyes wrenched at him. He turned away. "Never mind." He reached down and picked up the towel from the floor where he'd dropped it, feeling like the biggest idiot in the world.

* * *

After he'd talked to Special Agent Burrows, Trey snapped his phone shut. He rubbed his chin. "They found where he was staying, and he's gone. He's actually been there for three weeks." He shook his head. "Jesus, I don't know what the hell took them so long."

She smiled. "It wouldn't have taken *you* that long to find him."

He scowled. "Damn right. Anyway, they seem to think he's left town."

"That's good. Right?"

"Yeah. Except we don't know we're he's going now."

"He'll do it again. To someone else."

"Almost guaranteed," he replied thoughtfully. He opened his laptop and started going through files again.

"What're you doing?" She came to stand behind him.

"Just looking at things. Maybe something will give me an idea. Burrows thinks he may be going home to Brawley."

"What do you think?"

"It's possible. I'm going to check back with them later. They're checking some things out."

"What things?"

"His family." He sighed. "I went and talked to them months ago. Too bad I'm not still on the case; I think they'd open up to me if I talked to them." She watched his face and knew something was going on in his head. "Hey, maybe I'll take a little trip."

She stared at him, shaking her head slowly, her heart sinking. "To Brawley?"

"Yeah. And maybe El Paso."

"To see his sons?"

Trey looked up at her sharply. "How did you know he has sons?"

"He…um, he said that. That night. He was thinking of going to see them."

Dense silence filled the space between them for a moment. "You didn't tell the cops that."

She covered her eyes. "Oh, shit," she said on a moan. Her mind was all fuddled. "I don't think I remembered it until just now. When you said that." She looked at him again. "I didn't realize that was anything significant. Why is it important, Trey?"

Trey closed up his laptop and started throwing things into his suitcase. "He knows about them," he muttered.

She was confused. "What do you mean?" She trailed after him as he strode to the bathroom. "What you do you mean? He didn't know he had sons? I don't get it."

"His wife left him and never told him she was pregnant. Eleven years ago. She moved to El Paso to get away from his abuse, married again, raised the kids without them ever knowing about their father, or their father ever knowing about them. Until one day, her drunken mother spilled the beans to Barnes's mother. Just after he murdered Kathy Richards. Barnes called his mother after that and, for some reason, asked if she knew where Teresa had gone. When I went to see his mother, she'd just found out and she had no way to contact Sheldon, but I was pretty sure if she heard from him again, she'd tell him."

He turned to her his face hard, intent, bottles of shampoo and conditioner in his hands. "Is that all he said? What did he say that night?"

She thought back, her mind racing. She rubbed her forehead. "That's all he said. He acted like it was no big deal, like he was just going for a visit. He'd told Krista that he had two sons from a relationship a long time ago. Like it was all normal."

"He said he was going to see them?"

"Yes." She frowned, concentrated. "He said he was thinking about going to see them in Texas."

"Did he say El Paso? Did he know where they were?"

"Yes. Yes, I'm pretty sure he said El Paso. Or else when you said that, I wouldn't have immediately known that's what you were talking about."

He nodded and zipped up his bag.

"You're really leaving?" *What about me?* She was too proud to ask the pathetic, needy question. If Barnes had really left, she'd be okay. She'd go home.

He turned to her. "I wish I knew for sure he was gone," he said roughly. "I don't want anything to happen to you while I'm gone."

"I'll come with you." She was insane. Her business was disintegrating and here she was proposing to take off on a wild goose chase across the country.

"Marli, I can't let you get involved in this."

"You're just going to talk to his family, right? I won't get in the way." She blinked at him. "You know this is important to me. And I don't want to stay here alone."

He stared intently back at her. "Shit."

She hovered by him as he continued packing. "Are you going to fly there?"

"No."

"Why not? It's a long drive…"

"I don't have time to book flights and dick around in airports. And I don't have a bureau expense account any more. In fact, if they knew I was going there…"

"I can help drive, if you need a break. Can we go by my place to pick up a few things? I only grabbed enough clothes for one day yesterday. Or whenever that was. I'm all mixed up." She pushed a hand into her hair. God, she was babbling.

"Yeah. Let's go."

She was in.

When they got to her place, it felt like years since she'd been there. She missed her beautiful condo and all her stuff and especially her cameras. Trey followed her into the bedroom and when she threw open the closet door, he said, "Jesus Christ."

She glanced over her shoulder at him as she started pulling things off hangers. "What?"

He gaped at her overflowing closet. "Do you think you have enough clothes?"

She laughed. "No. I could never have enough clothes. Or shoes."

She stripped down, right in front of him, knowing he was watching, and put on fresh underwear, lacy red panties and a matching bra. She wriggled into a clean pair of jeans, shrugged into a snug tank top and pushed her feet into boots. She grabbed a tiny cardigan and thrust her arms into it, then started throwing some other things into her duffel bag.

"Okay," she said breathlessly. "I'm ready."

* * *

They were cruising on the freeway heading south toward San Diego, the sun glinting off the Pacific Ocean to their right. Marli lounged back in her seat. Other than the small knot of anxiety in her stomach that jumped every time she thought about what they were actually doing, they could have been on a vacation, or a weekend trip, a happy couple just getting away for a few days. She could pretend, but every time she looked at Trey's serious, forbidding expression she was reminded they weren't happy, and they certainly weren't a couple, despite the intensely intimate moments they'd shared.

"Maybe we should swing into San Diego for a couple of hours so you can see your family," she suggested, biting the inside of her cheek as she waited for him to blow.

He glanced at her, frowned, but admirably kept his cool. "Marli."

"What? I know you want to reconcile with them."

He just shook his head and concentrated on his driving.

"You're so cold," she said, trying again to push his buttons.

"Marli, not now."

"Well, when? We slept together, Trey. Doesn't that give me some rights to know a little bit about you?"

"Don't go getting any ideas about us," he bit out, not looking at her. "Yeah, we slept together, but I'm not looking for any kind of relationship. My life is fucked up enough right now."

Well, she'd gotten a response. Not exactly what she'd hoped for. Disappointment flooded over her, even though she'd known, in her head, that they had no future together. She pressed a hand to her chest and rubbed a little where her heart ached, and turned her head to look out the side window.

Trey's cell phone rang and he quickly answered it. After a brief conversation, he tossed it back onto the dash.

"Burrows?"

"Yeah. I didn't tell him where we were. He'd be pissed. Especially if he knew you were with me." He shot her a sideways glance.

"What did he want?"

"Last night Barnes stopped at the Honky Tonk Bar and Grill."

"Huh? How could he have? He was busy shooting at us."

"It was late. Two A.M. The place was almost closing, but he found someone to give him a ride home."

"No," she whispered, putting her hands over her mouth as she stared at him.

He shook his head. "He just took her car. Surprising, actually. Anyway, it does look like he's headed this way."

"Are…is the FBI officially chasing him?"

"They told me they're 'on it.' I'm going to call Bill again next time we stop and see what he knows. Or what he'll tell me."

She could hear the anger and frustration in his voice at not being in the loop on this whole thing.

"Trey, you won't get in trouble for doing this, will you?"

He was silent, but she saw his hands grip the wheel tighter. "If it all goes south, then hell, yeah. I'll be in deep shit. I may be anyway." He shrugged.

"Then why are you doing this?" He'd been away from his job for over six months, she knew. Why all of a sudden was he suddenly risking his career over this?

Could it be because of her? A faint hope grew deep within her that maybe he did care for her, more than he was willing to admit. What else could it be? After he'd rescued her that night, there was no reason he'd had to get involved. He could have just let the cops handle it and continued on his way up to San Francisco.

Of course, he was pretty serious about his career, and maybe he felt some kind of duty to finish off what he'd started. To stop a cold-blooded killer before more lives were lost. He was that kind of guy, and she loved it about him.

Oh, here we go again. She sighed inwardly. Thoughts of love and relationships had no place in her head, especially where Trey was concerned. He'd made that quite clear. She was going to get her heart stomped on, if she made it through this alive.

There was another pleasant thought.

"I don't know," he said.

"Huh?" She'd completely forgotten that she'd asked a question.

"I don't know why I'm doing this," he said, sounding almost disgusted with himself. And the tension in his big arms and hands as he gripped the steering wheel clearly said, Don't go there.

Don't go there. Don't go anywhere. Don't go anywhere near anything personal or emotional. She chewed on her bottom lip, pondering the mystery that was Trey. She knew so little about him, yet what she did know was huge. He was protective, dependable and trustworthy. He was honest and committed to doing the right thing. He hated to screw up. He was serious, but he did have a sense of humor. He was fantastic in bed. She grew warm just thinking about that. Even as a lover, he was generous, taking pleasure in giving pleasure, and boy, did he know how to give pleasure. Her nipples tingled and that low-down warm glow started between her legs again, so she forced her mind away from erotic daydreams.

She stared out the window, oblivious to the passing miles as the car sped along, thoughts racing through her mind just as quickly as the car was flying.

Trey was so closed off emotionally. He was complicated, no doubt about that. Something was causing him so much pain. She hurt for him and ached to be able to comfort him.

Someone had cheated on him. That much she knew now. It must have hurt him a lot, which meant he must have loved her a lot. Maybe, still did. A knife twisted inside her. *Damn.*

Her head leaned back, she stared out the window, images of last night running through her mind, wildly sexy thoughts about Trey doing carnal, erotic things to her. After a while, he glanced over at her.

"What are you thinking about?" he asked. "You look so intense."

"I was thinking about sex."

Trey choked. "Jesus, Marli."

"What? You asked."

He was smiling as he looked straight ahead out the front window.

CHAPTER 15

Once past San Diego, they turned onto Interstate 8 and stayed there for almost the next two hours. The flat highway stretched into the distance in front of them. Mile after mile of scrubby yellow desert passed by, the sky huge and wide and blue above.

"We'll stop in Brawley and talk to his mother," Trey said, glancing at his watch. "But I have this gut feeling he's headed to El Paso."

He was nervous about Marli being with him, for more reasons than one. He didn't want her to get involved in anything dangerous, although she already was. But, if they found Barnes, he wanted her nowhere near that psycho.

He was also worried about spending so much time with her in such close proximity. Her sexy body was driving him crazy, making him so horny he could barely see straight. Having her last night had just added fuel to the fire, increasing his hunger for her to the point of obsession. He had to have her again. And again. Sitting beside her in the vehicle was torturing him, testing the limits of his self-control.

It was more than that, though. She was clearly developing feelings for him that went beyond sex. He'd seen the phenomenon before—hero worship that got out of hand. Sure, he'd rescued her, but that was his job. So to speak. She was a strong, independent woman with a mind of her own and she didn't need him. The fact she was looking at him with soft eyes, worrying about his safety, and doing things like standing up for him to the FBI scared the hell out of him. Almost as much as Sheldon Barnes getting hold of her scared him.

He was in no position to have any kind of relationship with any woman, not with the mess his life was in hanging over him and no idea what to do about it. That would be so unfair to her. After the pain and betrayal he'd been through, he was definitely in no hurry to get involved again. Not to mention, his career was hanging by a thread. When he got back to work, *if* he got back to work after all this, he'd have to bust his ass to redeem himself.

He reached for the radio and played with the buttons until he found music without static. Country music. As soon as his hand returned to the wheel, Marli leaned forward and changed it, slanting him a wry smile. He shook his head, a grin tugging at his lips.

There was also the little issue of the night he'd been so close to getting Barnes and, because of his own drunken, self-pitying screw-up, had let him get away. Let him get away so he could go murder Marli's best friend. Knives twisted painfully in his gut, guilt and self-disgust churning in him.

Trey recalled exactly where Wanda Barnes lived and pulled up in front of the run-down bungalow on the edge of town. He looked at Marli. "You should stay in the car," he said, checking out the neighborhood. "Lock the doors."

Like locked doors would stop a madman with a gun.

She nodded, looking just a tad nervous. "I'll be fine." She lifted her chin.

He nodded back at her and got out of the car.

* * *

Sheldon liked driving. He had a nice sense of freedom when he was driving—open roads, no responsibilities, different views and things to see every mile, constantly changing, and all he had to do was sit there and drive. *Nice and easy. Yeah.*

He had a weird feeling. A feeling of inevitability. Like the end was near. But the end of what? Maybe he was going to die.

It had to end sometime.

He didn't like leaving Rocky Harbor without having gotten Marli, but there'd been too many close calls. His gut tightened, remembering. He'd never been especially careful, always felt invincible, had laughed at the goddamn FBI.

But now he knew he had two sons, he didn't want it to end yet. So he'd taken off. Stolen another car and hit the road.

Like he always did. Like after Cecelia in Montgomery. He fondly recalled meeting Cecelia.

She'd been pretty and petite, with light blonde hair, and he'd treated her well. He knew he could eventually get what he wanted if he got her hooked in with lots of compliments, pretty gifts and flowers. And it worked. They partied together and did the bar scene, and she was falling for him. He could tell. She let him fuck her the second time they met. He made it nice, slow and easy, so as not to scare her.

One night they were at the Ponderosa Bar and Grill with his buddy Dan and his girlfriend. Dan and Kim were apparently both horny that night, all over each other, kissing and groping. Sheldon watched them at first with amusement, then with arousal. He became aware of the boner in his pants and pulled Cecelia in for a big smooch.

"Hey," she said, pulling away from him, batting his hands away, "not here, Sheldon."

"Come on, honey," he coaxed, leaning over and sticking his tongue in her ear. "If they can make out in the bar, so can we."

"Sheldon," she said, "no."

He kept bugging her, tickling her, trying to kiss her. He knew she wanted it, too. She was just playing hard to get. After a while, Dan and Kim headed home. "Let's dance," Sheldon suggested, pulling Cecelia up onto the dance floor.

She went along with it, but when he tried to grab her boobs while they were dancing, she slapped his hands and stormed off the dance floor, leaving him standing there alone, humiliated.

Rage rose in him. He'd been doing so well since he moved to Montgomery. Cecelia had been nice to him, did whatever he wanted, never laughed at him, so things had been going good. But now she'd pissed him off.

The anger bubbled up in him like boiling water in a pot, and he struggled to put a lid on it. Sometimes he didn't really want to put a lid on it. Sometimes he just wanted to let it boil over. Sometimes he just wanted to do something that showed just how angry he was.

"Let's go," he said tersely, back at the table. He grabbed Cecelia's hand and dragged her out of the dark bar.

"Hey, Sheldon," she complained, whining a little, "you're hurting me."

He clenched his jaw, but said little as he got into the driver's seat of Cecelia's white Toyota. He drove them to her place, a small apartment above a convenience store. Cecelia had a roommate, but she was out.

Even when she did come in later that night, she wouldn't disturb them. She knew Sheldon stayed over all the time.

"Take your clothes off, bitch," Sheldon ordered Cecelia in her bedroom.

She looked at him warily, but her fingers went to the buttons of her blouse and she started to disrobe.

"You're scaring me, Sheldon." She removed her blouse and then her jeans. He saw it, then—the fear. In her eyes. Making her fingers tremble. And the rush of supremacy shot through him, a burst of adrenaline that made his blood surge.

"Yeah? Well, maybe you should be scared." Maybe he'd just fuck her hard and then he'd feel better. His hands went to the button of his jeans.

She stood there in her bra and panties. "I don't think I want to do this if you're in that kind of mood." She was shaking now and pushed her hair off her face, fright making her eyes dark.

Blood roared in his ears, his heart banged like a drum and his vision narrowed to Cecelia, standing there half-naked, trying to challenge him, even though she was terrified. When he grabbed her and forced her to the floor, twisting her wrists and making her cry out in pain, the exhilaration was incredible. The power and her pain combined to give him a high like he'd never experienced.

The next day, Cecelia's roommate had found her stabbed to death on her bed and her car keys stolen from her purse.

Sheldon smiled at the memories, then glanced at his watch. He was near Brawley. He should go see his folks, but damn, he was still pissed off they hadn't told him about his sons. Never mind that they'd just found out themselves. Never mind that they had no fucking idea where he was, so they couldn't tell him.

He needed to take a leak, so he pulled into a gas station. He needed gas, too, but, hell, his wallet was nearly empty. He eyed the self-serve pumps and checked for security cameras. *None.* He grinned.

After he used the bathroom and spent his last few bucks on a can of soda and a bag of chips, he filled up his tank, then jumped into the stolen car and pulled away.

He laughed the next five miles down the highway.

That job at the saloon hadn't been bad. He'd made some tips, but too bad they'd actually expected him to work. He popped the top on the soda and gulped some down, the sweet fizz stinging his throat. He didn't mind work. Sometimes. He just wanted to work when he felt like working. His job at that ranch had been the best gig he'd ever had.

He saw a sign for the Chocolate Mountains, which reminded him of the first person he'd ever killed.

He still was kind of surprised at how easy it had been to kill the old man. Ed shouldn't have tried to stop him. He should have just let him take the stuff and go, and then he wouldn't have had to do that. Sheldon shrugged as he drove, remembering. Holding the gun at Ed and seeing the fear in his eyes had given him quite a rush. Quite a rush.

But he knew he couldn't kill him right there, so he'd tied the old guy up, taken his car and driven them up to the old man's cabin in the Chocolate Mountains. Tied him to a chair. He felt like a god when he'd pointed that loaded gun at Ed's head and seen the terror there. He grinned again. He'd felt powerful. He'd never felt a rush of power like that in his life. The only other time he'd ever felt anything close to that was when he'd forced Teresa to do things to him that she didn't want to...when he'd hit her or tied her up to make her cooperate. She'd had that terror in her eyes, too, that used to turn him on and make him feel strong and in control. Just thinking about it sent a thrill through him again.

Too bad Teresa had taken off. They'd gotten married young, but the marriage hadn't lasted long. He didn't know she'd gone to El Paso and gotten married again. *Whore.*

He finished the cola and tossed the empty can onto the floor of the passenger seat. She'd had his sons, let another man be their father, and never even told him. Teresa should pay for that. *Yeah.*

* * *

Wanda Barnes was home and so was her son Peter, two years older than Sheldon. Peter was a convicted criminal, too, in and out of jail, probably dangerous, but he'd never murdered anyone.

"We ain't seen him," Peter told Trey. He folded his arms across his chest and tipped his chin up.

Wanda's eyes shifted back and forth between them as she twisted her fingers together. She shook her head in agreement. "But he called me again," she told Trey, earning a dirty look from Peter. "A few weeks ago."

"Mama!"

"He said he didn't do nothin' wrong," she told Peter. She turned back to Trey, her faded blonde hair streaked with grey, her thin face looking far older than he knew her to be. "And I believe him. I'm worried about him."

"If you're worried about him, you should tell him to turn himself in," Trey advised her gently. "Otherwise, something really bad could happen to him." He held her gaze as he said it.

"I know. I've seen all the stuff on the news." Her voice trembled. "They'll kill him."

Trey nodded slowly. "You told him about his sons, didn't you?"

She shot him a nervous but defiant glance. "Yeah. He deserved to know he's a father."

"You ever think he might try to see them? That he might be angry at Teresa for not telling him about them all these years?"

She gripped the fingers of one hand with the other. "You think he might hurt them?"

Trey shrugged. "Sheldon has a problem controlling his anger, doesn't he." He said it like a statement, not a question, but she nodded slowly and put a hand to her mouth.

"Someone should tell Teresa."

Trey nodded. "I don't know for sure if that's where he's going, but it's sure possible." He gave her a card. "Will you call me if he shows up here?"

She took the card, but Peter grabbed it away from her and ripped it in half. "You're a cop. You're not trying to help Sheldon. Quit trying to make her think you are."

"Sheldon has killed a lot of people," Trey said, his voice hard. "He's dangerous. He could be dangerous to both of you and he could be dangerous to Teresa and her kids. Whether you believe it or not, I'm looking out for you and anyone else he might get it in his head to kill." He stared at Peter, then turned back to Wanda. "You don't have to call me. Just call the police if you see him or hear from him again."

He turned and went back out to the car, finding Marli sitting in stifling heat, the windows all rolled up, doors locked. Her face, drawn into tight lines, cleared as she saw him.

"So?" she asked the instant he got in.

He started the car and drove slowly away before he told her what had transpired. He was scoping out the neighboring houses, just looking for anything…anything at all.

It was almost seven o'clock. "We can find a place to stay here," he told Marli. "Or keep driving. We can be in Tucson before midnight."

"I don't want to stay here." She shivered. "I'm not getting a good vibe from this place. It's too small, and I feel too conspicuous."

"Fine." Trey had no problem with that whatsoever. "We need gas and food. Once we get away from Brawley, we'll find somewhere to stop, then we'll head for Tucson and spend the night there."

CHAPTER 16

They drove through the dark for hours. Marli convinced Trey to pull over so they could trade places and she drove for a while. She thought he might doze off like she had earlier, but he stayed alert and tense the whole time.

"Why did you become a cop?"

"My dad's a cop," he reminded her. "I just always wanted to do that. The criminal mind always fascinated me. I wanted to get inside their heads and figure out why they did the things they did. The satisfaction of catching a criminal, prosecuting him, seeing him convicted is amazing. It's exhilarating."

"You love it, don't you?"

"I guess. Yeah. I'm pretty committed."

She shot him an amused glance. "I'm guessing that's an understatement. You're so intense, you probably don't even have a life outside of work, do you?"

He looked uncomfortable. "Maybe."

"Do you have a life outside of work?"

"I don't have much of a life, period," he said quietly. "Not right now."

The curiosity and desire to know what was making him tick burned fiercely inside her. He was so closed off to her, so tightly wound she was afraid at some point he was going to explode.

"You're very...moral, aren't you?"

"What does that mean?" he asked. "Of course I have morals."

"I mean, you want to do the right thing. I don't know what you did that you consider so heinous, but you don't like to make mistakes, do you?"

"Nobody likes to make mistakes."

"True. But I think it bothers you a *lot.*"

"Yeah." His voice was low.

"And you have pretty high expectations of other people, too, don't you?"

He was silent, staring out the window at the passing scenery. What was he thinking about? She didn't bother asking him, like he'd asked her earlier, because she knew he wouldn't answer.

* * *

He was thinking he'd like to change the subject.

"How about you," he said. "Why photography?"

She considered that. "It's always been something I loved. Capturing images… I can't paint or draw, but I have this *need* to capture beautiful things, for other people to see. My work isn't important, but it's a way for me to do what I love and actually earn a living. The stuff I do for myself is more creative, I guess. But I also love the technical part of it, the science of it, getting the light right, the exposure, knowing how to translate the image from real life into a photograph that captures it for eternity, does it justice. Does that make sense?"

He nodded. "I think so. You must be good at it."

She shrugged. "I do okay." She glanced at him. "I'd like to photograph you."

"Huh? Why?"

"Your face is so interesting…complex. All those shadows and secrets. But when you smile, you light up like the sun coming out from behind a dark cloud. It's almost breathtaking."

Whoa. Was she talking about him? Clearly, this was a woman who saw things others didn't.

"We're both so lucky," she said musingly.

"Why's that?"

"We both get to earn our living doing something we love."

Lucky. Huh. He hadn't felt lucky for a helluva long time.

* * *

When they neared Tucson, they found a decent-looking motel with a vacancy sign.

Inside the quiet, dark motel room, Trey dumped their bags on the floor in the corner. He turned and looked at Marli. She was stretching, arms over her head, her body arched, head back, tits thrust out. Her tank top rode up and revealed her flat belly and the flash of her diamond piercing. *Oh, man.*

She'd gotten inside his head, somehow, inserted herself in there, and somehow she knew stuff about him he wasn't sure he knew about himself. It was kind of freaking him out. Preferring to deal with the physical rather than the emotional, he went over to her and yanked her against him, roughly, pressing his hard cock into her softness, and kissing her with a bruising, demanding kiss.

A startled sound escaped her, and her hands came up to clutch his shoulders to regain her balance, but then she was kissing him back, just as demanding, winding her arms around him, arching into him. The hunger simmering in him boiled over, and he ground his mouth into her, tongue thrusting inside, taking her with hot urgency.

She had him throbbing everywhere, hot, jolting desire shooting through him. The edginess and tension that had gripped him all day, the pent-up need and adrenaline that had built up in him while he was forced to sit in the confines of the goddamn car all day, rose up in him. His heart was pounding, his ears roared, he had to have her.

His body clenched, craving Marli and the release she could give him. His hands gripped her ass and lifted her against him, and he ground his pelvis into her, hard and horny.

"Trey!" she gasped against his mouth. "Take it easy."

"I can't," he muttered, nipping at her bottom lip, sucking it into his mouth. "I can't. I'm burning up. Christ, I need you, Marli." He fisted his hands in her hair, yanked her head back and kissed her again, ruthlessly taking her mouth, parting her lips wider.

She gave a small whimper, but she didn't retreat. She clung to him, pressed herself into him as if she couldn't get close enough, one long leg wrapping around his calf. He reached down and grabbed that leg, lifted her thigh over his hip, thus giving him better access to the softness between her legs, and he thrust himself there, his dick so hard he thought he might burst.

"Now," he bit out. "I need to fuck you. *Right now*."

He flicked open the button of his jeans, then let go of her to lower his zipper, thrusting his pants and boxers down past his hips. His cock sprang free, hard, red, throbbing. Then he had Marli's jeans open, too, and pushed them down to her knees. She kicked them off just as he grabbed her ass again and lifted her against him, taking two steps and slamming her against the wall.

She gave a soft gasp, and he covered her mouth with his again as her legs wrapped around him. She folded her arms around him and held on, and he inserted a hand between them to find his cock and shove it into her.

"Trey!" She wrestled her mouth away from his. "We need a condom."

Shit. He paused, gasping for breath, eyes closed. "Yeah. Okay, yeah." He searched his memory and, with immense relief, recalled putting a condom in his pocket. He shoved a hand into his jeans, hanging just off his hips, and pulled it out triumphantly. He handed it to her and, behind his neck, she ripped it open and dropped the wrapper. Between them, they managed to get it on him without Marli falling to the floor, and then he was in her again, hot and hard, thrusting in and up, powerful, fiercely pounding into her.

Her head thunked against the wall as he drove into her, her eyes closed, mouth open. He pressed his face into the side of her neck, gave her a hot, wet love bite there, then inhaled. Then his climax crashed over him and he exploded in her, his hips jerking between her softer ones, and she cried out, her fingers digging into his shoulders in a pain that was strangely satisfying.

His body slowed and then stilled, pressing her against the wall, as he dragged air into his lungs.

"Jesus, Trey." She moaned. "You are so over the top."

He took one more breath in, then lifted his head. "Did I hurt you?"

She rolled her head back and forth against the wall. "No. Yes. I don't know. I've never been fucked up against a wall before."

Her words turned him on all over again and made him shudder. "You didn't come," he said tightly. "I'm sorry."

"I think you know what to do."

She never ceased to amaze him with her honest forthrightness. He couldn't help but smile, his face hot and tight.

"Yeah," he said. "I know what to do." Holding her luscious ass cheeks, he stepped away from the wall. His pants almost tripped him up, but luckily the motel room wasn't big and it was only a few steps to the bed. He tossed her down and she bounced on the mattress with a little squeal. He kicked off his jeans, ripped his shirt off over his head and knelt between her legs.

"I've been dying to taste you again." He parted her thighs, this time with more gentleness, but still with focused intensity.

She shivered and fisted her hands in the bedspread. He leaned in for a taste, a long, luxurious lick, a suckle, a nip. She writhed beneath him, drenched and swollen with her arousal, thighs quivering. The scent of her filled his head—warm woman, her taste like melting honey on his tongue.

He ate at her with insatiable hunger, using his lips and tongue to torment her, bring her up. She arched into his mouth, cried out and went over the edge, vibrating in ecstasy.

He lifted his mouth from her pussy and sat up, wiping his chin.

"There," he said with satisfaction, taking note of the dazed look of pleasure on her face. "That should take the edge off. Now we can take our time."

"You can't possibly—"

He tossed the used condom somewhere toward the waste basket across the room and slid up beside her on the bed.

"Let's get under the covers." He tugged back one corner of the bedspread. Marli rolled away from him, lifted herself up, then rolled back under. She was still wearing her T-shirt and bra, and he carefully pushed the shirt up, then lifted it over her head, deftly snapped open the closure of her bra and tugged it off her, revealing her perfect breasts. They were exactly how he liked breasts—full, round, with high nipples. He leaned down and took one in his mouth, sucking gently on it, wringing a low moan from her.

He wanted to hold her for a few minutes before he made love to her again. He pulled her against him, loving the way she fit herself to his body. Their legs twined together in an instinctive dance. They stayed like that for a while. He could feel her heartbeat, her every breath, like it was his own.

A vague feeling of uneasiness stirred in him. The emotions he'd been repressing earlier were teasing his consciousness: a feeling of tenderness for this woman, a feeling of connection, a faint, growing buzz of vitality.

He closed his eyes and pressed closer to her.

CHAPTER 17

They might have slept. The lamp glowing in the corner provided the only light, and Marli found Trey's broad wrist and turned it so she could see his watch. It was nearly two in the morning, but time had basically stood still since they'd entered that room.

He taken her so fast and hard her head had spun. Was still spinning. But she'd loved it, loved every rough, hard thrust of his body, his fingers digging into her soft flesh. She'd likely be bruised and sore tomorrow, but she couldn't care less. She loved that she could provoke such strong emotions in him, this man who was so tightly controlled and self-contained. It was in him. She didn't know exactly what "it" was, could only hope, but she knew he had *some* feelings for her.

She snuggled closer against him, his body radiating heat and energy. His hair-roughened legs were tangled up with hers, and she slid one leg up and down, rubbing him. He stirred against her, his thick penis twitching, and she ran her hands down his smooth back.

They moved together, slowly, languorously, rubbing against each other. She found his mouth, their heads on the pillows, and they kissed as if they were drunk, long, slow, open-mouthed kisses, in perfect unison. A yearning grew in her, a hunger for him, a deep, empty ache low in her belly, between her thighs.

With one leg over his hip, her pelvis moved rhythmically of its own accord, instinctively circling, pressing, lifting against his big thigh. Their mouths still joined, their bodies moved together in small, languid pulses that gradually became hungrier, hotter.

He rolled her over onto her back, pressed her down, kissed her deeply, full-mouthed, his tongue sliding in, filling her mouth. She was lost to it, drowning in sensation, her body dissolving, melting, liquid heat pooling lower in her belly and making her ache for more.

His hands were everywhere, on her breasts, tugging her tender nipples, stroking her belly, her thighs, tickling, making her shiver. Then he was turning her again, onto her stomach, gently.

"Trey…"

"Shhh. I didn't finish exploring you last night," he said softly. "I didn't finish finding all those little places that make you shiver, all those places you love to be touched." His hands were magical, and she moaned as they roamed over her back, dipping into the curve of her spine, then sliding over her buttocks, cupping and cuddling them, stroking between them, sliding down to the backs of her thighs.

Oooh. She let out a long sigh of delight, his hands caressing her thighs. She'd had no idea she was so sensitive there, that she could derive so much delicious pleasure from being petted there.

Her legs moved a bit on the bed.

"I knew I'd find more places," he murmured, and bent to kiss her there, on her thighs, her rounded cheeks. He nipped, making her gasp, then licked, his tongue warm and velvety. "You're so responsive…you love to be touched, don't you, sweetheart?"

She murmured her agreement. *Oh, yes.* She loved to be touched, just like that. His hands were big, a bit rough, finding every spot on her body that thrilled her. The intense aching need between her legs grew, pulsing and throbbing, begging to be filled, hunger spiking in her sharply. Excitement built and twisted within her, and she tried to turn over, but Trey's big, hard hand pressed on her lower spine, holding her down. A thrill jolted through her, making her almost desperate with need.

She whimpered, face pressed into the mattress, the sheet soft beneath her cheek. She put her index finger into her mouth and sucked.

She heard Trey's sharply indrawn breath when she did that, but she was a mindless, aching glow of need. She lifted her butt against his hands, parted her legs a little and his fingers slid into her from behind, into her wetness. He pushed inside her and it felt so, so good, but it wasn't enough.

"Fuck me, Trey," she whispered, eyes closed, butt lifting against his hand. "Please, fuck me."

With a ragged groan, he rolled away from her and off the bed, desperately searching out the condoms he'd packed. She waited, hips still moving involuntarily, seeking fulfillment.

When he came back, she expected him to take her from behind again. She'd loved it when he'd done that, but instead, to her surprise, he turned her over, easily lifting her pliant body. She looked up at him, his dark face intent and hungry.

"I want to see your face," he told her. "I want to watch you while I fuck you and make you come." He shuddered at his own words, then positioned himself between her thighs. He took his weight on his elbows, the muscles in his powerful shoulders bunched, he pushed into her, and, God, it felt good, so good, like he was completing her, filling her with what she was missing.

He filled her right to her very core, touching deep inside her, sliding in and out with a delicious friction that built and built. She focused on it, tightened her inner muscles around him, rubbed against him with every down stroke, seeking, reaching...With an intense, spiking pleasure, she shattered, riding wave after wave of heat and ecstasy.

She cried out, clutched his back, his tight muscles flexing and rippling as he kept stroking in and out of her, every stroke sending aftershocks through her sensitive womb, until he came himself in tight, pulsing jerks.

He kept his eyes on her, his jaw tight, head back, as he poured himself into her and the connection between them was like a palpable thing, their eyes locked in a moment of profound intimacy, their bodies fused.

They stayed like that for long heartbeats, breathing heavily, unable to take their eyes off each other.

When Trey finally moved off her and rolled to his back beside her, she turned to him and touched his face. "I love you, Trey," she whispered.

His eyes closed, his face taut, he laid there, chest rising and falling as he still labored for breath.

"You shouldn't do that," he finally said.

Her heart sank and a chill shivered over her.

"I'm sorry." She rolled away from him and perched on the edge of the bed. After a moment, when she started to shiver, she fumbled around in the tangled bed clothes and pulled them up under her chin, staring at the wall with blank eyes.

Trey got up and disposed of the condom, clicked off the lamp and got back into bed, not touching her, not saying a word.

* * *

In the morning, Trey's gaze was dark and shuttered as they got up and packed their belongings. He checked them out of the motel and they stopped at a nearby Denny's for breakfast.

The thought of eating made Marli want to vomit. Her stomach churned. She shouldn't have told Trey she loved him, but that's the way she was. She couldn't *not* tell him. It was too important.

But he was such a stupid idiot. He *did* have feelings for her; she *knew* he did. He couldn't have made love to her like he had last night if he didn't care about her. She'd seen the emotion in his eyes after they'd watched each other come—the heat, the tenderness, the connection. She'd *felt* it.

And now, although parts of him had always been closed off to her, he was totally aloof and cool. He snapped out orders to get in the car, put on her seatbelt, hand him his coffee. She seethed with irritation at his high-handed control, but also at his stubbornness and the ridiculous boundaries he'd set.

They were in El Paso by early afternoon and, once again, Trey seemed to know exactly where to go to find Sheldon Barnes's sons. He stopped in front of a small but neat house in northeast El Paso. The neighboring homes were all similar in size, some of them neatly kept, others more run down. Children played outside, and a lady sat on the front steps of one house watching them. It wasn't an affluent neighborhood, but seemed clean and safe.

Marli looked around as Trey prepared to get out.

"I know, I know," she said. "Just go."

He looked at her long and hard, his face inscrutable, then opened the door and slid out. The minute it closed, Marli pressed the button that locked all the doors with a clunk. Trey went up the front sidewalk.

There was absolutely nothing to be afraid of on this warm, sunny fall day in a friendly El Paso neighborhood, but once again her nerves were frayed. Trey was acting like such a jerk, she wondered how she ever fell in love with him. Her chest ached. She shivered and wrapped her arms around herself, looking nervously toward the house Trey had just entered. She wondered if any of the kids playing two yards over were Sheldon Barnes's sons.

No, those kids were too young, only about four or five years old.

She watched him knock on the front door and wait. And wait. Nobody was answering. He disappeared around the side of the house. It seemed like forever, but the clock on the dash had only measured a few minutes when he returned.

"She's not there."

He sat in the driver's seat, silent.

"Now what do we do?"

Trey drew in a breath and looked out the window. "Talk to the neighbors. Come on."

She followed him up to the house next door to Teresa's. Nobody home there either. They went on to the next one, where the children were playing, and the woman sat on the steps watching them. Her plump curves stretched a T-shirt and shorts.

"Hi," Trey said with a charming smile.

Marli pursed her lips. He could pour it on when he had to.

"We're looking for Teresa Fisher. We're old friends from out of town. Do you know where she is?"

The woman looked at him. "She's gone. She packed up and left last night."

Trey conveyed surprise. "Where'd she go? On a vacation?"

"Uh…maybe. She didn't tell me where she was going. I just saw her loading the kids and their stuff into the car last night."

Trey smiled. "What time was that?"

She studied him. "Just after the kids got home from school. About four, four-thirty."

"Darn. I guess we just missed her. Thanks, ma'am."

He took Marli's elbow and directed her back to the car.

He sat in the car for a moment before he started it. She looked at him, but said nothing.

Then he glanced at her. "He was here."

"How do you know that?"

"Just a gut feeling. Why else would she pack up and leave like that? Maybe Wanda Barnes warned her Sheldon was coming. Or maybe he showed up and scared the hell out of her."

"At least she's still alive."

"We hope." He looked grim. He rubbed his face.

Marli bit her lip. Now they seemed to be close, her uneasiness was growing. And the fact Trey was so distant and cold didn't help. All along, his big, comforting presence had made everything bearable. She wasn't sure if she could do all this without his reassuring support.

She took a breath. She had to get through this.

"So what do we do now?" she asked, trying to keep her voice cool and steady.

"Damned if I know." He pulled away from the curb and drove slowly down the narrow street, mindful of the kids playing.

"If he was here, we just missed him," he said thoughtfully. "He didn't get that much of a head start on us." After a moment, he said, "He must've shown up in the afternoon, while the kids were at school. I bet he'll be back. That's why she's afraid. He probably wants to see the kids."

He stopped at a stop sign, then made a right turn. "I need to think." He drove down a street lined with strip malls and fast food restaurants. "I'm trying to remember where her husband works. She told me. Damn. Usually I remember everything."

"It'll come to you."

"Yeah. Let's get some food." Trey pulled into the parking lot of a donut shop.

They stood in front of the counter, eying the pastries.

Marli sighed. "I'll have a coffee and a glazed donut."

The woman working there filled a cup, plucked a donut out of the case and slipped it into a paper bag. She looked at Trey.

"Uh, coffee and…pecans."

Marli blinked. He turned to her and flashed a grin. "Pecans. He works at a pecan factory."

It took her brain two seconds to realize he was talking about Teresa Fisher's husband. She laughed. "The cinnamon pecan roll reminded you?"

"Yeah." Still smiling, he ordered one of the sweet rolls, then pulled a few bills out of his pocket to pay.

"Let's eat in the car."

He booted up his laptop, perched on the console between them, while they ate their snacks and sipped coffee. Then his fingers flew on the keyboard as he searched various engines and finally found it. "The Texas Pecan Company." He made a disgusted noise. "I couldn't remember *that*?"

"You have the address?"

"Yup. And directions how to get there." He closed the computer. "Our next stop."

Marli expected a big manufacturing plant, but the pecan company operated out of a small brick building.

"This is good," Trey said as they walked to the entrance. "If it was a huge place, they'd have security and might not even know him."

He asked at the reception desk, and the woman working there paged

Barry Fisher. A few moments later, a man appeared in the small lobby, wearing a beige uniform. "Hi," he said, eyes wary. "What can I do for you?"

Marli let Trey explain who they were and ask if there was somewhere private they could talk. Barry led them reluctantly into a small office.

"Yeah, he showed up yesterday," he confirmed, hands rubbing together. None of them elected to sit in the office chairs. His eyes darted between Trey and Marli. "He scared the shit outta Teresa."

"Did he see the kids?"

"No. They were in school. Teresa told him to come back after supper, but she got the hell out of there before he came back."

"Where'd she go?"

Barry looked at them. "I'm not telling you that."

Trey nodded. "Okay. Is she safe?"

Barry nodded.

"Any idea where Barnes is now? Where he stayed last night?"

"Nope. No idea. I hope to hell he left town."

Trey shot a glance at Marli. *Damn.* They knew he'd been there now, but this wasn't helping find him.

"Anything you think of, let me know, okay?" Trey handed the other man a card. "We just want Teresa to be safe."

Barry nodded, his mouth a thin, unhappy line, eyes shadowed. "Okay."

Back outside in the baking parking lot, Trey and Marli paused.

"What now?" she asked him.

He said nothing, just stared hard, one hand on the frame of the car door. "Let's head back to the Fishers' neighborhood. If Sheldon's anywhere in El Paso, that's where he'll be."

"I could use a bathroom."

"Oh, sure. I need gas again. Keep an eye out for somewhere."

As they neared the Fisher home, Marli pointed out the Happy Pumper station, and Trey turned in, pulling up to the self-serve gas pumps. "Go on in," he said curtly. "I'll fill up."

She went into the gas bar and convenience store. Racks of junk food, soda and magazines crowded the small space. A couple of customers were paying for gas, chips and cigarettes. The gas station attendant behind the counter looked barely old enough to be working there.

Marli spotted the sign for the bathroom and went down the short, narrow hall, carefully locking the door behind her. She turned up her nose as she looked around. Not the cleanest place, but she had to pee, so it would have to do. She carefully lined the seat of the toilet with toilet paper before perching on it.

She scrubbed her hands clean and then, thinking about maybe getting a coffee if it didn't look too bad, she walked out of the restroom. A man came down the hall toward her, and she glanced at him as she moved to her right to go around him. He looked familiar. Where did she know him from?

It was the bartender from Cactus Jack's. He'd been serving her Diet Cokes for the last few nights. What was he doing here in El Paso?

Their gazes met hers and recognition flashed in his eyes, too. Those eyes…

Oh. My. God.

Marli stared at him in shock and then she saw it—the tattoo on his arm. A lasso.

CHAPTER 18

The world froze around her and her limbs felt heavy and stiff. With a fearful little squawk, she started to rush past him, but he put out an arm and easily stopped her.

"Hey." His other arm came around her and, to her horror, she saw he had a gun in it.

She started trembling uncontrollably. "Trey!" she tried to cry out, but the man's arm cut across her throat. It hurt, and all that came out was a hideous gurgle.

"Well, well, Marli," Sheldon Barnes said, "I can't believe my luck. I'd just given up on you."

She reached up and clawed at the arm squeezing around her neck.

"No, no, don't," he said, waving the gun. "You'll get hurt."

A sweat broke out, dampening her forehead, stinging her underarms. Her stomach churned, the coffee and donut she'd eaten earlier threatening to come back up. What on earth did he think he was going to do to her? Frantic thoughts ran through her mind. There was no way out except the front door. They had to go back into the store. There were other people there. They'd see them. He couldn't do anything in plain sight of other people.

Yes, he could, her nearly hysterical inner voice said.

Calm down, calm down, she chanted in her mind, her gaze bouncing wildly around.

Apparently, Sheldon had come to the same conclusion she had. Either he was going to drag her into the bathroom and rape and murder her, or he was going to have to go out through the store somehow. And Trey was out there.

Please, please, please, Trey, she silently begged him. Save my life…one more time.

Maybe he heard her.

There he was. She could just see him walking up to the counter, pulling his wallet out of his back pocket to pay for the gas. The attendant said something to him.

Sheldon saw him, too, and he turned and shoved her in front of him, back down the dingy hall. He pushed her into the men's room, and she almost stumbled and fell on the grimy floor. She put a hand out and it flattened on the tile wall, cool and smooth.

She turned, shaking, lungs taking in shallow breaths.

Sheldon slammed the door shut and locked it, then turned to her with the gun in his hand. It gleamed dully in the flickering fluorescent light.

Her body tight, she stared at him and blinked.

"What are you doing here, bitch?" he inquired conversationally. "Don't tell me you're looking for me." He grinned, and she almost vomited at the evil she saw. "Got you that hot for me, huh?"

He took two steps across the small room, and Marli moved, the porcelain of the urinal cold against her arm. She cringed.

Sheldon grabbed a handful of her hair and tugged. "You pissed me off that night, you know?"

She shook her head, closed her eyes. She could smell him…a mixture of stale body odor and mint chewing gum. She swallowed, her throat constricted. What had she done to piss him off?

"Yeah. You did. You laughed at me." He yanked on her hair and her head jerked back and cracked against the tile wall. She whimpered.

Then she sucked in a long breath, opened her eyes and glared at him. "Let go of me, asshole."

He laughed. "Oooh, scary. I knew you were a real ball-breaker."

"What do you think you're going to do now, Sheldon?" She fought to keep her voice steady. "You're trapped in here. Trey will come looking for me. He'll call the police." *Please, Trey, please.*

What if she never saw Trey again? She loved him, the big, stupid jerk. What if she never got to tell him what a special man he was…never got the chance to say goodbye? What if her last words to him were "I have to go to the bathroom"?

He turned his head away from her and nodded. "Yeah." He thought for a moment. "We have to get out of here. Come on."

He unlocked the door, poked his head into the hallway, then reached back and fastened his fingers around her wrist.

He pulled her out into the hall. Her gaze flew to the front of the store, where Trey was sliding his wallet into his back pocket. She tried again to scream and this time a louder noise came out. She kicked out and managed to hit Sheldon in the shin with her booted foot, causing him to curse loudly.

"Shit! You bitch!"

Trey looked up and the way his face changed so quickly to a look of shock and horror amazed Marli in some deep recess of her mind. She tried again to wrestle Sheldon's arm away from her, figuring if she was going to die anyway, she might as well go out fighting.

"Stop!" Sheldon commanded her harshly. He put the barrel of the gun against her temple and dragged her down the hall toward Trey. "Back off!" he shouted to Trey.

She'd seen Trey instinctively reach for his own gun, but he stopped himself, seeing the gun at Marli's head. He'd lost all color in his face and his eyes glittered darkly, his mouth pressed into a straight, grim line.

"Let her go," he told Sheldon. "You're done, Sheldon."

"Who the hell *are* you?" Sheldon asked. "You've been in my way for days now. I said, *back off*."

"I'm a cop," Trey said softly. "Don't shoot me, Sheldon. You'll be in even bigger trouble than you already are."

"I don't care anymore. You're right—I'm done."

Oh, shit. Shit, shit, shit, was all Marli could think. She stopped struggling, the hard gun against her temple more terrifying than anything she'd ever experienced.

CHAPTER 19

Shit, shit, shit.

Marli's huge, terrified eyes pleaded with Trey, an arm wrapped around her throat, and a gun held to her head. It had to be Barnes, but he did look different. *Wait.* Suddenly, it clicked into place. *Shit.* What a fucking *idiot* he was.

After stopping completely when he first saw Marli, Trey's heart was now about to pound its way out of his mouth, galvanizing tension gripping him. He was acutely aware of everything around him—the frightened eyes of the young kid, the little grey-haired lady standing there holding a quart of milk, the cool draft from the fan in the ceiling above him. He heard the thin, scratchy music playing on the radio behind the counter. Then reflexes kicked in. His heart rate slowed. His senses, eyes and brain began to work in synchronicity as he called on every bit of training and every professional skill he'd ever learned.

A guy who didn't care if he lived or died was not going to negotiate. Sheldon had nothing to lose by killing.

Trey glanced at the kid behind the counter, who also looked wide-eyed and terrified. "Get down," Trey ordered him.

The kid dropped to the floor. One other customer stood in the small store.

"Sheldon, I'm telling this lady up here to leave. She doesn't need to be here. Okay?"

"No!" he shouted. "Nobody leaves!"

"Okay," Trey said calmly. "She's just going to go behind the counter here." He grabbed the small lady with grey hair and pushed her down with the kid. "Now let go of Marli, and you and I can talk."

"Fuck off! There's nothing to talk about."

"Sure there is." Trey kept his voice low and calm. "You don't want to die, do you?"

He watched Sheldon's face as he struggled to think, decide what to do.

"You just found your sons, Sheldon," Trey reminded him softly, taking his eyes off Sheldon only long enough to glance at Marli. She was shaking like a poplar in a windstorm, but she was holding herself together. "You don't want to die now. Just tell me what you want. I'm a cop. I can help you."

"Yeah, right. You're not going to help me."

"I can help get you what you want," Trey said patiently. "Just tell me what you want."

Sheldon said nothing, his breathing shallow and noisy.

"Do you want to run?"

"I'm done running."

"Yeah," Trey said. "I guess you're tired of running."

Again, Sheldon said nothing, but Trey knew he was listening, thinking. He'd planted the possibility of escape in Sheldon's mind and taken his mind off killing Marli.

"Let her go," Trey said. "And I'll let you walk out of here."

"I said, I'm tired of running!"

"But you have two boys to live for," Trey reminded him. "Don't you want to see your sons?"

"They don't even know me," Sheldon said. His hand with the gun in it was shaking a bit, making Trey nervous, but feeling like he was making progress. A trickle of sweat ran down his back. It would be okay. It had to be okay. If he fucked this up… *God.*

"That's hard, eh?" Trey said sympathetically. "But they'll be out of school in a few hours and you can finally see them. I bet you'll be proud of them."

"That whore Teresa should've told me she was pregnant," Sheldon snarled.

"Yeah, she should've." Trey paused. "I talked to your mom earlier. She's worried about you."

"I saw her on TV last night, telling me to turn myself in."

Trey was surprised. Maybe his visit had had some impact. "Are you thinking about doing that? It's what your mom wants."

Sheldon was silent, obviously struggling with his thoughts.

Confidence seeped into Trey. He could do this. Sheldon was losing his focus, and Trey just needed the opportunity and a distraction. He glanced around the store, then found Marli's eyes.

The sight of the terror there undid him, but she lifted her chin, firmed her lips, met his gaze. She was so fucking brave.

Then Trey saw something out of the corner of his eye. Through the window. A cop car had just pulled up outside. Did they know Sheldon was in here? Trey sucked in a breath, hoping they weren't going to fuck things up.

He focused on Sheldon, trying to watch the cops with his peripheral vision.

"She doesn't care about me," Sheldon said bitterly. "She never cared about me."

"Why do you say that?" Trey kept a wary eye on the cop car outside the building. No one was coming in, and he wasn't sure if that was good or bad.

"She tried to kill me," he said. "So many times."

It looked like he had loosened his grip on Marli a little. She still looked terrified, but was taking everything in, staying calm. Trey moved a little closer to Sheldon.

"Like what?" he asked.

"Like when she locked me in the closet," Sheldon snapped. "She left me there for *two days*. And the time she got pissed off at Peter and me and took us out to the dunes and left us there. She left us there, all alone, with no food or water. It was over a hundred fucking degrees."

"What did you do?" Trey asked, sidling a little farther along the counter.

Sheldon again was silent and his hand had dropped away from Marli's head. At that moment, the front door of the store opened and a uniformed cop appeared. Sheldon's gaze swung sharply to the door and instinctively he shifted the gun, aiming toward the cop who'd stepped in.

Trey launched himself at Sheldon. Marli cried out. The gun blasted.

CHAPTER 20

Trey and Sheldon crashed to the floor, knocking over a rack loaded with bags of potato chips. Trey grabbed for Sheldon's right hand holding the gun. He shoved Marli hard and she went down, too, behind them, but she was free. Adrenaline rushed through Trey's blood, fueling his muscles, and he used every fiber of his being to wrestle with Sheldon. The guy was big and strong, though. Panting and determined, Trey fought, finally managing to grab the bastard's right wrist and twist it sharply, forcing the gun to drop. His vision focused only on the man in front of him, but at the edge of his sight, he saw a slim, booted foot kick the gun away. It skittered across the worn linoleum floor.

"Freeze!" called the cop, gun drawn and leveled right at them.

Trey drew back his arm with one last desperate move and drove it into Sheldon's nose, blood spraying, his head bouncing back hard on the floor. Then Trey wearily sat back on the floor, while two other cops ran over to Sheldon.

Then Marli was on her knees beside him, tears running down her face, tension and fear etched in her beautiful features. She was touching him all over, crying, saying his name over and over.

He turned to her in a daze, adrenaline still pulsing through him.

"Are you okay, honey?"

She laughed through her tears, shakily. "No," she said. "No, I am definitely *not* okay."

With concern, he turned to her, framing her face with his big hands. "I'm not hurt," she told him, still touching him compulsively. "I'm just…just…a little stressed."

He groaned at her egregious understatement and grabbed her, pulling her onto his lap, wrapping his arms around her, tucking her head under his chin.

"Are you okay?" she mumbled into his chest. "God, Trey." She picked up his right hand to examine his knuckles, but they were just a bit red and scraped.

"I may have a few sore muscles later, but right now I don't feel a thing," he said truthfully.

They watched in bemusement as the cops cuffed Sheldon Barnes and led him out to the police car.

Trey stood up, pulling Marli with him, and went over to make sure the gas station attendant and customer were okay. They were both in shock, barely able to speak. And they didn't even know who Sheldon was. They just thought he'd been robbing the store.

They talked to the cops. "How'd you guys know he was here?" Trey asked them, flexing his hand.

"Teresa Fisher called in this morning to tell us he'd been there yesterday looking for money, wanting to meet his sons. She told them they were at school and gave him thirty bucks. Told him to come back after."

Trey nodded. They knew that much.

"Her husband called her and told her you were looking for him, and she realized she had to do something. She gave us a description of what he was driving and we spotted his car as we were patrolling."

"Jesus, that was lucky."

"Trey, you'd have got him anyway," Marli said softly. "You were awesome." She paused. "That was some football tackle."

Trey identified himself to the cops. "Hostage rescue training kicked in," he said. Thank God, Sheldon had still had that faint hope of meeting his kids. Otherwise, negotiating with him would have been next to impossible. He swallowed hard and tightened his grip on Marli's waist.

Much later, when they'd finished with the police and all the news media, they sat in Trey's car, both of them staring a bit blankly out the window.

"Is it really over?" Marli asked wonderingly.

"Yeah, honey, it's over. What do you want to do? Start driving back tonight? Or we could get a room here and leave in the morning."

"I want to go home," she said. "I want my life back. I want to go to work, have lunch with my friends, go shopping." She wiped a tear off her cheek, glancing at him.

"We can start driving," he said. "See how far we get and then we'll stop for the night."

"Okay."

* * *

Nearly seven hours of driving later, Trey exited the highway and drove into the parking lot of a Hilton resort near Phoenix.

"We're staying here?" Marli looked at the huge, luxurious resort.

Trey nodded.

"This is beautiful," she said, "but we don't need to spend all this money just for a place to sleep."

"We're not going to just be sleeping," he told her, and a little thrill of excitement ran through her. "Besides, we're celebrating."

"Oh. Okay."

They checked in and went to their room. It was even nicer than Trey's room at the Rocky Harbor Inn, beautifully decorated with a soft plaid blanket draped over the fluffy white duvet on the king-size bed. French doors led to a balcony overlooking the huge pool area, complete with a waterfall flowing over elaborate boulders. A bouquet of fresh sunflowers sat on the gleaming wood dresser.

"We can go down and have dinner in the restaurant," Trey said.

"It looked pretty swank. Can I at least change?" Not that she'd brought much to change into. She did have one skirt, a denim one that ended at mid-thigh. She put it on with a black camisole top and the little cardigan, and, with her sparkly flip-flops, it didn't look too bad. She wished she had her whole closet to choose from, wished she could dress up in something pretty to impress Trey.

Trey was looking at her legs when she turned to face him, and warmth pooled low in her belly at the heat in his eyes. Since the face-off at the gas station, he'd been jolted out of his cool detachment, and the heat had been building again between them with every mile they'd traveled.

They walked into the elegant restaurant and the hostess showed them to a table for two in the corner. A candle flickered on the table, real flowers sat in the vase, and the waiter whipped her linen napkin out of the stemmed goblet and handed it to her. She smiled up at him and looked at Trey across the table.

"After all that's happened, this is surreal," she said. "It's like we're on a date. We've never done that."

"No."

He met her eyes and the air became charged with sexual electricity.

"Maybe we should've just had room service," she said, her voice thick.

His eyes warmed. "You look gorgeous. As usual. Supermodel gorgeous."

"Supermodel!" She gave a little laugh. "Hardly. Remember, I work on the other side of the camera?"

"It's those long legs of yours," he said. "They turn me on."

"Oh. Well, good." She took a sip of the water the waiter had poured into her glass, then opened the thick, leather-bound menu.

She looked it over and snapped it closed.

"That was quick."

"I'm not very hungry."

He lifted a brow, but kept reading his own menu. Finally, she opened hers again and quickly made a decision.

He ordered a bottle of wine for them, also something they'd never done, and they drank wine and talked, mostly about what had happened that day.

"I can't believe I never realized the bartender was him," Marli said, shaking her head. "He was right there in front of us the whole time."

"Sort of. And, hey, I was just as stupid. I should've recognized him, too. He never spent a lot of time with us, though. Most bartenders are pretty friendly types, but I remember noticing one time that when I wanted to order a drink, he practically ignored us. He must've been nervous about you recognizing him."

"But the tattoo…" Marli said. "That's what clued me in that it was him today. I should've noticed *that*."

"I didn't really pay much attention to him," Trey said thoughtfully. "But I'm guessing he was wearing long sleeves while he was working."

"And how did he get a job there anyway?" Marli demanded.

"Probably used a different name and fake ID. He's done it before."

She shook her head. "I never would have thought that." She sighed. "God, Trey, when it all clicked into place, I just about died."

"Ha. *I* just about died when I saw him holding you like that. Christ." He shook his head, eyes full of remorse. "I will never forgive myself for putting you in that position." He cursed. "I shouldn't have brought you into such a dangerous situation."

"Oh, Trey." She sighed and smiled. "You beat yourself up over everything. I didn't exactly give you much choice about bringing me. And I'm fine. Everything is fine now."

He didn't look convinced.

"You really were amazing," she told him again. At the time, she hadn't recognized what he was doing, but now, in retrospect, the way he'd stayed so calm, talked to Sheldon, got his guard down was so impressive. "How did you know what to say to him?"

"Hostage rescue training," he said. "Part of my education. I did some work as a crisis negotiator for a while, too. I like getting inside the heads of criminals."

"That's scary." She shuddered.

"Nah. It's fascinating. Anyway, I knew I had to get him thinking about escaping, otherwise, there was nothing to negotiate with. If he didn't care if he died, he had no reason not to kill you. Or any of us, for that matter. Thank God he hadn't seen his sons earlier, so he still had some reason to want to escape."

She shivered again. "We should really stop talking about that. Enough."

"It's important to debrief," Trey told her seriously. "It helps. You've been through a hell of a lot the last few days. Weeks."

She nodded slowly and sipped her wine. It was making her feel a little warm, a little relaxed, but she was still edgy and aware of Trey sitting across from her, all big and gorgeous and brave.

"You saved me. Again," she told him solemnly. "How can I ever repay you for that?"

"It's not something you have to repay," he said roughly. "Don't be crazy."

She shook her head. "I can't even get my head around it all." She paused. "Maybe I can't repay you, but I can show you how grateful I am." She met his eyes meaningfully. "Later."

His eyes glittered with desire and his white teeth flashed in a smile. "Okay."

Trey feasted on herb-crusted prime rib, and Marli picked at lobster ravioli. They skipped dessert and went back up to the room. They meandered out onto the spacious balcony and stood at the rail in the cool night air, enjoying the view of the deserted pool glowing turquoise in the dark.

Trey turned to her, eyes dark and mysterious. "Marli..."

She faced him, studying him. "Yes?" Her heart beat with

anticipation at what he was going to say. Surely, now he realized he cared for her.

"I'm sorry." He stopped.

Everything in her wilted with disappointment. Even so, when he put his hands on her shoulders, she felt that pull, felt her soul inexorably drawn to him. Her body yearned for him despite her disappointment.

"Don't," she whispered and went up on her toes to brush her mouth across his. "Don't say anything, Trey. Just, please, make love to me. Because we're here and we're alive. You don't have to make any promises."

He drew back and searched her eyes. He could probably see all the love she felt for him, and she lowered her lashes, before she kissed him again. Heat exploded between them, and he gathered her into his arms in a crushing embrace, kissing her with fevered intensity. She surrendered to him totally, in a sweet, hot rush of passion, wrapping herself around him.

They stumbled through the doors back into the room and stood beside the bed.

"Undress me," she invited him huskily, standing before him.

He slipped the single button of the cardigan open and pushed it off her shoulders, then lifted the camisole over her head. Her bra was also black and he flicked the front opening and pushed it off, too.

Then he went to work on the button and zipper of the denim skirt and worked it down over her hips, leaving her standing there in black lace panties that were a band of lace around her hips.

"I want to leave these on," he murmured, kissing her softly, his fingertips tracing over the lace and around to the back where it half-covered her butt cheeks.

She shivered.

"My turn," he said, dropping his arms.

She smiled and unbuttoned the two buttons of his polo-style shirt. She ran her hands over the thick, soft cotton and the hard, sculpted muscles beneath. She tugged the shirt out of his jeans and slipped her hands under it onto fever-hot skin. She pushed the shirt up, hands on his chest, and bent down to press a kiss right in the middle of his chest. Then she pulled the shirt over his head and dropped it to the floor.

His jeans came off next, falling to the floor, heavy with his wallet and change. She had no inclination to leave his underwear on, wanting to see his arousal, wanting to feel it…taste it.

She dropped to her knees on the soft carpet and slid her fingers under the elastic of his snug boxer briefs, tugged them down over his long legs and off. He stepped out of them and planted his feet apart, standing before her, his erection blatant and impressive.

She studied him, admired him. "Beautiful," she murmured, taking him in her hands and caressing him.

He groaned.

She curled her hand around him. He was amazingly soft and hard. The tender tip of his penis was velvety, but underneath he was like steel. She traced the throbbing veins and, as she clasped him, she could feel his heartbeat, fast and strong.

She pressed her face to the crease where his thigh met groin and inhaled the scent of him, warm and musky and so intimately *him*. Her tongue gave a little lick there, kissed him, and his thighs quivered.

He parted his legs a little wider, and she slid one hand through and behind to capture his balls, fondling them, squeezing gently, bringing more moans and muttered curses from him.

"Yes," he said with a groan, his whole body tight.

Then she took him in her mouth, swirling her tongue over the head, wetting him, tasting him, trying to swallow him.

"Oh Christ!"

She made love to him with her mouth, sucking and squeezing him, cupping his heavy sac, loving how it tightened in her hand. She wanted to make him come, wanted him to spill himself into her mouth. His hands came to her head, gentle at first, guiding her forward, then with increasing urgency, pushing harder, faster.

"Yes, like that." He groaned. "Harder… Oh, Marli!" He cried out her name as he came, pulsing in her mouth, the hot, sharp taste of his semen a triumphant, extravagant delight for her mouth.

She sucked and licked him dry, slowly released him and sat back, then licked her lips. She gazed up at him.

His face looked stunned, flushed, full of gratitude and awe. He fell to his knees on the carpet in front of her and gathered her against him, buried his face in her hair. She kissed his shoulder and hugged him back.

"Good God," he murmured, "I think my legs just gave out."

Then they were lying on the floor tangled around each other, hands greedily groping and touching, mouths meeting in long, clinging kisses, trying to consume, devour, inhale each other.

"God, Trey," she gasped, climbing on top of him.

He clasped her hands, and she lowered herself onto his hot, hard shaft, riding him. Their fingers curled and tightened around each other's, and she surged and rose on him, pulling at him with every inner muscle she had.

"Condom," he growled. "We need a condom. I can't last…especially bareback, like that."

All she wanted was him inside her, and at that moment she couldn't care less about protection, but he lifted her off with his hands on her waist and set her aside so he could go get a condom.

He was back in an instant, already sheathed, and rolled across the carpet with her, then inside her. He moved over her, looked down at her face, and the tenderness in his eyes almost brought her to tears. He touched her hair, pushed it off her face, pulled one strand from her mouth. He leaned down and kissed her then, thrusting into her with long, slow moves, touching deep inside her, and she came, hard, fast and sharp, startling her. It was intense, almost painful. He swallowed her cry, heaved against her, hips driving, pumping.

"I'm coming, Marli," he told her, voice low and rough, then he was pressing into her in hot, heavy pulses, and she came again, this time longer, softer waves of heat that slid down her legs and made her weak.

She couldn't move, couldn't breathe.

She held his big, heavy body tightly, stroked his damp back, the curve of his tight butt, his thick, powerful shoulders, fighting back tears. God, she loved this man with all her heart. She choked on the words that wanted to escape from her, swallowed hard, her throat aching.

He buried his face in her neck, breathing hard. She so much wanted to hear him tell her he loved her, and squeezed her eyes shut as she hugged his body.

* * *

Trey rolled away to drop the condom into the wastebasket, then rolled back to look at Marli, all sexy and naked and tousled. "Come on," he said, taking her hands and pulling her to her feet. He drew back the covers, and she crawled between them. He slid in, too, and pulled her against his chest.

"So what happens now?" she whispered.

"We go to sleep." But he was afraid that wasn't what she meant.

"No, I mean to us."

He tried to come up with the words to tell her without hurting her, but he wasn't very good at that kind of stuff. "There *is* no us."

She immediately looked down, shuttering her eyes from him. She plucked at the white sheet wrapped around them. "I know." She lifted those beautiful eyes and pinned him with her gaze.

"Will you at least tell me what happened to you, Trey? Before we go back to our own lives. If nothing else, it really does help sometimes to talk about it. It hurts me to know you're hurting. Maybe I can help."

He looked at her long, his heart thudding in his chest. He wanted to. He owed it to her, and she was right. He needed to talk. He'd been to see that counselor the bureau had sent him to, but it had been too soon, and he'd been resistant to having his head shrunk.

He reached behind him and propped the pillows up so he was sitting. She snuggled against him, all warm and naked, sliding one leg across his thighs.

God, where to start. "About seven months ago, my wife told me she was pregnant."

Marli tensed and started to draw away from him. He held on to her as she tipped her head to look up at him. He swallowed at the stunned hurt on her face.

"You have a wife and a child?"

CHAPTER 21

Seven months earlier
San Diego, California

"Hey, guess what?"

Trey's partner, Bill, looked up. "What?" he asked, a donut halfway to his mouth.

Trey grinned. "Lisa's pregnant. We're gonna have a baby."

Bill's mouth dropped open, then his face split into a huge grin. He dropped the donut, jumped out of his chair and went over to slap Trey on the back.

"That's fantastic!" he said. "Congratulations!" Happily married, with two children, Bill was the kind of guy who thought everyone should be married with children. "When is she due?"

"August," Trey said. He rubbed his face, but smiled. "It was a bit of a surprise, but what the hell." Little by little, he was getting used to the idea of being a father. He pictured himself with a son, playing baseball, taking him to Padres games. Or maybe a little girl. He wasn't sure what he'd do with a girl, but, hey, maybe she'd play baseball, too. He grinned.

"I never thought I'd see the day," Bill said. "Wasn't sure you had it in you."

"Screw off." Trey grinned. "Come on, we've got work to do. I'm off to Brawley today."

They'd been immersed in the Sheldon Barnes case for weeks,

desperate to find this guy before he killed again. Trey had gathered so much information on Barnes he felt as if he knew him better than he knew his own brother. They didn't technically call it profiling since they were field agents, not profilers, but that's what he was doing. He wanted to know what made this guy tick, what gave him an adrenaline rush, because Trey sure got a rush from figuring out what went on in a psychopathic, narcissistic murderer's mind.

In Brawley, he met Sheldon's mother, Wanda Barnes, a thin, tired-looking woman. Her hair was faded, but he could tell it had once been a pale gold blonde, just like the three women victims.

"He called me the other day," she told Trey nervously. "For some reason he wanted to know if I knew where his ex-wife is."

"Sheldon was married?"

Wanda nodded. "Her name is Teresa. Teresa White. They got married when they were only seventeen. She was a mousy little thing—her father had just died and her mother was falling apart. I think she thought Sheldon would look after her." She gave a sharp, mirthless laugh. "Guess she found out pretty quick that wasn't gonna happen, because she just up and disappeared one day."

"Where'd she go?"

Wanda shrugged. "I never knew. Never cared. But after Sheldon called, I went and paid a visit to her ma." She scowled. "That woman's a mess. Hammered all the time. But she says Teresa's living in El Paso. And…" She hesitated.

"What?" Trey probed gently. He met Wanda's eyes with reassurance.

"Debbie White says Teresa has two kids. Eleven-year-old twins." She frowned. "Teresa's married to someone else, but it was eleven years ago she was married to Sheldon."

"You think the kids are his?"

Wanda shrugged, still frowning. "Jesus, I don't know. But if they are, Sheldon deserves to know about it."

"Did you tell him?"

Wanda shook her head. "I don't know how to get hold of him."

"Are you going to tell him? If he calls?"

Wanda's mouth twisted. "You're just full of questions, aren't you? Hell, I don't know if I'll ever hear from him again."

"You will," Trey said confidently. "You will."

Trey went next to visit Sheldon's older brother Peter in the nearby state penitentiary, then talked to cousins and other relatives in the

Imperial Valley area and found out Sheldon had occasionally shown up looking for money or a place to stay. He traveled to El Paso to talk to Sheldon's ex-wife as well. The two boys had never met their father, their mother having fled her relationship with Sheldon when she was pregnant. She'd never known if Sheldon knew about the boys, but figured he didn't, since he'd never showed up looking for them. She, too, hadn't seen him since then, and had been horrified about the news stories she'd been seeing on television. Horrified and frightened.

"You need to know his mother will probably tell him about his sons," he cautioned her. "There's no reason to think he'd come here, or that he'd have any intention of harming you. But..." He couldn't help but eye her flaxen hair.

Trey had decided to drive all the way back to San Diego that night, rather than stay over in a hotel, and arrived home after midnight to an empty house. Where the hell was Lisa? A four months pregnant woman out partying? Weird.

He grabbed a beer and wandered into the bedroom. The computer monitor was still on, so Lisa must have been doing something on it earlier. He touched the keyboard, the screensaver disappeared and her e-mail program appeared. He reached for the mouse, intending to close it and shut down the computer, but his eyes were drawn to rows of e-mails from the same sender...

Travis. Why was his brother Travis e-mailing Lisa so much? His eyes scanned the list. There were five e-mails today alone, several from yesterday, three days ago and more.

Trey gnawed on his bottom lip, then tipped the beer to his mouth. He should close the program. That was Lisa's personal e-mail. But as he lowered the beer with his left hand, his right hand slowly moved the cursor up to the top e-mail and clicked. The message opened.

If you're sure Trey won't be home tonight, you can spend the night with me, he read. *It would be so awesome to sleep with you all night.*

Trey swallowed hard with disbelief, his heart squeezing painfully in his chest. The room went out of focus and the beer dropped from his fingers to the floor, foaming all over the pale grey wall-to-wall carpet.

When Lisa walked in the next morning, her mouth dropped open in shock to see him there.

"How long has this been going on?" he demanded.

He hadn't slept all night. He'd tortured himself by reading e-mail after e-mail, including the ones she'd saved. He already knew the answer to his question. Their affair had been going on for nearly three months.

"How could you do this? And with my own *brother*! Jesus!"

Lisa started to cry. He watched her, afraid he was going to cry himself, feeling hollow and frozen inside. Not only was his marriage done, but his own *brother* had done this to him. Never mind Lisa, how could *Travis* have done this to him? Hot knives of pain and betrayal sliced through him.

"I'm sorry." She sobbed, dropping onto the bed and covering her face. "I'm sorry, Trey."

He just stood there, feeling like the biggest sap in the world. *What a fucking idiot.* Why hadn't he seen this? He shook his head.

"We're having a baby," he whispered painfully. "How could you do this to our child? How could you, Lisa?"

She only sobbed louder.

"Lisa?"

Her muffled sniffs and choking gasps were her only response. Cold terror gripped him. "Lisa, tell me I'm the father."

She moaned. Trey's gut roiled and he thought he might actually vomit. The world stopped for a long, painful moment.

"Jesus Christ, Lisa. For the love of God, please, tell me you're not pregnant with Travis's baby."

She raised her face to look at him. She was a pretty woman, but right now her face was blotchy pink and puffy and she looked more miserable and distraught than he'd ever seen her.

"Are you really four months pregnant?"

She shook her head.

Fuck. No wonder she still wasn't showing.

"No," he choked out. "No." He turned around sharply, unable to look at her, afraid he actually might physically harm her, his rage was so great. He clenched his hands, eyes squeezed shut while his heart pounded painfully in his chest. "Son of a bitch!" He drove his fist into the wall, shattering the drywall and leaving him with bleeding, throbbing knuckles.

Lisa gave a startled whimper behind him. He flattened his hands on the wall and lowered his head, sucking in air.

He'd already packed his things. He had nothing left to say.

He worked incessantly. There was nothing else left in his life. His wife and unborn child—ha! What a joke. His wife, his unborn *nephew*, his brother were all dead to him. He couldn't face his sister or his parents and their own feelings of betrayal and pity for him. Just could not face it.

He moved into a furnished studio apartment not far from the bureau and buried himself in the Sheldon Barnes case. He studied and restudied every detail until his head swam. Still, people were reporting sightings of Barnes, although he seemed to be lying low. Which was unusual for him. It did seem to indicate he was still in the area, though.

Cops had staked out Sheldon's family home in Brawley, thinking he might return there, but he hadn't. At least, not yet.

When Trey wasn't working, he was drinking. Too much, he knew, but he couldn't bring himself to care. He made strict rules about not drinking on the job, only permitting himself to drink himself into oblivion after he'd left work.

One night he stopped at a bar instead of going home, unable to face one more lonely night in that cold, bare apartment. He needed some noise, some people around him, even though he had no desire whatsoever to talk to anyone.

He sat at the bar at the Pinto Club, chugging back beer after beer. Happy couples twirled on the dance floor, laughing, and he watched them with detached interest. A burst of laughter from a nearby group drew his eyes for a moment. A group of women at a table were laughing about something apparently hilarious and having a great time.

Trey ordered another beer and sighed. The empties lined up in front of him told him it was time to go home. Only problem was, which he hadn't thought of earlier, he was probably too drunk to drive. Not that he felt drunk. He felt stone-cold sober. Nah, that wasn't true either. The room had taken on a bit of a fuzzy glow.

He could easily walk the few blocks to his apartment. With that thought, he tossed back the remainder of the beer and lifted a hand to signal the bartender for another. *What the hell.* If he had to walk home, might as well have a really good reason. And the alcohol was finally starting to make him feel pleasantly numbed to the pain that was constantly with him.

The laughing group of women caught his eye again. One of them was getting up to dance. A man led her onto the dance floor, a good-looking guy with shaggy blond hair. The woman, too, was blonde, a long sheet of platinum hanging down her back. They danced well together, a snappy two-step, and when the song ended, they returned smiling and breathless to the table. The man pulled out a wallet and tossed bills onto the table, then wrapped his arm around the woman.

Apparently, they were leaving, waving good-bye to her friends, weaving their way across the bar to the exit. As they passed by Trey, he got a look at the man's face.

Trey's reflexes were slow due to his excessive alcohol consumption and it took a minute before he realized Sheldon Barnes had just walked past him. Escorting a woman out of the bar.

Trey jumped unsteadily to his feet. *Shit. Shit, shit, shit.* He started after them, knocking a chair over in his inebriated haste. People were looking at him, but he didn't care. Adrenaline kicked in. He stumbled out of the bar into the dark parking lot and saw a brown Ford leaving.

"Shit!" he yelled, and ran for his own vehicle.

His heart was going to explode out of his chest. He grabbed the cell phone clipped to his belt and made the urgent call for back-up. Even as he stabbed the key into the ignition, he knew this wasn't a good idea, but desperation and determination to stop that psycho killer, to save that woman from God knew what, overrode his common sense.

He squealed out of the parking lot, trying to keep the Ford in sight. They turned left at the first lights and he followed, narrowly missing an oncoming vehicle that blared its horn at him as it swerved. *Fuck.* He pressed on the gas pedal, trying to catch up to them, trying to talk on the cell phone, trying to focus on the road ahead of him.

"I'm on Market Street," he yelled. "Coming up to Park Boulevard. He's about two blocks ahead of me."

There was too much traffic. He blinked, trying to clear his vision, and pulled out to pass the vehicle in front of him that was impeding him. He pulled into the oncoming lane just as a Jeep Liberty turned from a side street right in front of him. The lights blinded him and with wrenching metal, exploding air bags and squealing tires, the collision was head-on.

CHAPTER 22

The words came out a lot easier than he'd expected. "I wasn't sure if I was ready to have kids, but, hey, it'd happened, so I was kind of getting used to the idea. Actually"—he gave a mirthless little laugh—"I'd started to look forward to it. It was kind of cool."

Marli was still studying his face, and he pushed her head down against his chest, unable to bear the pity he knew he'd see in her eyes. "It was pretty tough," he said, in outrageous understatement. "My marriage was destroyed, I was no longer going to be a father, and my brother had betrayed me. That was almost the worst thing. It was humiliating, even at work. People felt sorry for me. My family was devastated. They were pissed at Travis, which they should have been, and they felt sorry for me and it was brutal."

"It must've been." Her fingers moved on his shoulder in warm, comforting circles.

"I was hurt, angry, sad. I was so furious, I was mad at the whole world, not just Lisa and Travis."

"Oh, Trey. How do you possibly get through something like that?"

"Not very well. I was stupid. I didn't give a shit about much, except for catching Sheldon Barnes. I worked all the time and like I told you, if I wasn't working, I was drinking." He paused. "I could almost numb the pain with enough booze."

"Did he…kill her? The woman in the bar that night?"

"No. Lucky for her, she got away. But…" He couldn't say it.

"What about the people in the other car? Were they okay?"

"Yeah, lucky for them, too. But I got suspended from my job, lost my license for six months, went through torturous rehab. When my suspension was up, I could drive again, so I bought a new vehicle I couldn't really afford and decided to take one more month and go see Kent in San Francisco. 'Course, I never made it there."

"Oh, Trey, you've been through hell." She was silent, stroking his shoulder softly. "Is this the first time you've talked about it?"

"Basically, yeah. The bureau sent me for counseling, but it was too raw to talk about it back then. I had no one else to talk to. I couldn't face my family. I wasn't going to work, and that was fine because it was humiliating just to see the look of pity on everyone's face."

His marriage was over, but there really had been no closure. He'd never spoken to Lisa again since that night, even though she had now given birth to his brother's child. Lisa was irrevocably a part of their family, whether married to him or not, whether he liked it or not.

He'd gotten the e-mails and voice mails from his family, telling him he now had a nephew, but he'd never responded to them. Didn't know what to say. Couldn't bear to see the pity in everyone's eyes, couldn't face Travis who was now a father to what should have been *his* baby. He waited for the familiar ache in his chest that always accompanied that thought. But it wasn't there. *Huh.*

"And you still haven't talked to your family about it?"

"Christ, no. Don't you see what a fucking mess it is? Lisa had the baby a month ago. He's part of our family. *She's* part of our family."

"But you're divorced, right?"

He hesitated. "Um…no. No, actually."

* * *

Marli went very still. "Oh."

She'd been sleeping with a married man. She was *in love* with a married man. She drew away from him, taking the sheets with her to cover her nakedness. She pushed back and sat up.

"I went to see a lawyer right after it happened," Trey explained. "He was going to start working on the divorce. Then all that other shit happened and I just didn't care enough to bother with it."

"Oh," she said again. "Were…are you hoping you two will get back together?"

He ran an agitated hand through his hair and leaned his head back against the headboard. "Christ, I don't know."

That was *so* not the answer she'd wanted to hear.

She wanted to hear an emphatic "No!" Not that ambiguous response. Her heart hurt so bad she couldn't breathe.

"Well, your trip to San Francisco didn't turn out so well," she said lightly. "I'm sorry about that."

"God, Marli, don't."

"Well, it is my fault. Although, you could've just left. I never really understood why you stayed around."

He closed his eyes. "Don't you see, Marli? Krista would still be alive if I hadn't fucked up that night and let Barnes walk right by me."

She turned to stare at him. "You blame *yourself* for Krista's murder?" *Wow.* She turned that concept around and around in her mind, looking at it, thinking about it. "Hey, buddy, that's *my* turf."

"You don't have the market cornered on guilt," he said wearily.

She nodded. Well, that sort of explained it. Once he'd found out what was going on, guilt had made him stay and try to fix things.

Just like she'd been trying to do. She knew only too well the power of guilt to make you do stupid, irrational things. It was almost funny, and she started to laugh, but it was hollow laughter, her throat burning, eyes stinging.

"You are such an idiot." She stabbed a finger into his chest, and he looked at her in surprise. "Yeah. You are. You already told me Krista's murder wasn't my fault. What the hell are you thinking, feeling responsible?" She smacked his shoulder. "Jesus, how stupid can you be?"

His eyes went wide with shock. He stared at her speechlessly.

"I guess you expected me to be all sorry for you. Poor Trey. Well, I'm not. You're acting like a big baby."

"What!"

"You are. Wallowing in self-pity, running away from your problems. You haven't dealt with your wife, your brother… anything. And you won't deal with me."

"What the… That's bullshit."

"Think about it, Trey." She glared at him. "I love you. I know you care about me."

"Don't love me," he shouted. "I'm not worth it. Look at me!"

She gave him a long look, her heart tight in her chest. "I'm looking at you. And I'm seeing a man who is strong and caring and protective, someone you can count on, someone who saved my life. More than once."

"That's not what you said a minute ago," he muttered, shifting his eyes away from hers. "Marli, I have nothing to offer you. Who knows what's left of my career after all this. I'm married to another woman; my family is a mess. Christ."

"I know. But I love you anyway." Her lips twisted. "Don't worry, Trey. I'm not going to cry, or beg, or stalk you or anything. But you need to know how I feel. I'm sorry if you don't like it."

"Oh, Christ, Marli, don't."

Her chest rose and fell with each long, painful breath she took as they stared at each other.

"I thought when you found out how I screwed up and let Barnes get away, you'd be mad at me. Hate me."

She slowly shook her head, frowning. "I'm not mad at you for that. How could I be?" She could imagine his pain, his suffering after finding out the child he was looking forward to having with his wife was that of another man, his own brother. Fury rose in her toward his brother and his wife. How could they have done that to him? And then, he'd tried to save that woman in the bar. Sure, he'd screwed up, but he'd been trying to save a life.

"You were hurting," she said. "You weren't even working that night. You were trying to do a good thing, but you made a mistake. Everyone does."

He shook his head, looking doubtful.

"You told me it's not my fault that Krista was killed," she said. "Well, it's not your fault either. It's Sheldon Barnes's fault." She poked him in the chest. "*His* fault. *He's* the murderer. Not me. Not you."

They stared at each other for a long moment, but suddenly she was overcome by exhaustion, limp with fatigue, heavy with despair. "We should get some sleep."

Once again, she rolled to the edge of the mattress and pulled the covers up to her chin.

When she woke up in the morning, she and Trey were plastered against each other, hot and sticky, his hand holding hers tightly beneath his cheek as he slept. She watched him, a deep, aching sadness squeezing her heart until his eyes flickered and he awoke, too.

When they'd packed and checked out, he said, "We can pick up some food on the way." He tucked his credit card back in his wallet.

"I'm not hungry."

"You need to eat." He took her bag from her and led the way to his car.

Bossy as usual.

It was a long, quiet drive back to LA.

* * *

When they arrived in Rocky Harbor that afternoon, Trey took her first to get her car. After she got out of his vehicle, she turned, leaning on the door. "You don't have to come back to my place. I'm good from here."

"I'll make sure you're home safe," he said, not looking at her.

She shrugged and slammed the door shut, then walked over to her own car. He followed her home and pulled into her driveway behind her.

She unlocked the front door, disarmed the alarm system she'd almost forgotten about, and dropped her purse on the table. Trey came in behind her and set her bag down. She turned to face him, smiling brightly.

"I'll take this upstairs for you," he said.

She started to protest, then relented. "Thanks." He climbed the stairs.

She wandered around her condo. It was such a relief to be home. It would be a while before she felt normal. Hell, after everything that had happened she would probably never feel normal—or how she used to feel, anyway. Things that happen change a person, she reflected, trailing a hand over the shiny granite counter in her little kitchen. Having your best friend brutally murdered. Having a psychopath try to kill you. Falling in love… Those were all definitely life-altering events. She sighed.

"So." Trey was back. "Get that back door fixed."

"Yes, sir!" She saluted him, and he rolled his eyes.

Her smile faded. He was leaving. She knew it.

Her heart hurt, felt like it was cracking wide open in her chest, so painful she almost couldn't breathe. They stood there looking at each other, and she fought the tears stinging her eyes.

"Just go!" she finally burst out and turned her back on him so he wouldn't see the tears spill over. He came up behind her and put his hands on her shoulders. She shrugged them off. "Please, Trey, don't drag this out. It's killing me."

"I'm sorry."

Not only was she heartbroken, she was pissed. How could he be such an idiot? She swiped her hands across her eyes. "Just go. If you're not man enough to deal with your problems, if you're too chicken-shit to admit your feelings, I don't want to be with you."

He went very still behind her. She immediately regretted her words. Hell, it was the truth. Blunt. Honest. If it hurt his feelings—ha! Like he had any feelings—too bad for him. Why should she be the only one in pain?

She turned to him, looked at him for a long moment, searching his eyes, studying the strong line of his jaw, the firm lips that could look so forbidding but give so much pleasure, the rough, dark stubble on lean cheeks, his short, dark hair standing in all different directions from running his hands through it. At this moment her biggest regret was she'd never photographed him and would only have memories of his image.

She put her hands on his face, feeling his rough warmth, and he closed his eyes and turned his mouth into one palm, kissing her there.

The pain was agonizing, the sweetness of his touch almost beyond bearing. She swallowed a sob, and he leaned down to kiss her mouth, softly, tenderly. She opened for him, drank him in, touched her tongue to his to taste him one last time. Then he touched her cheek and leaned his forehead on hers for a brief moment.

"I love you," she whispered.

Then he was gone, and she slumped back against the counter, feeling like her heart had just been ripped out of her chest.

CHAPTER 23

Trey'd been back in San Diego, back in his ugly, bare, rented apartment with its drab furnishings, for two days. It seemed like years since he'd been there, but it was only a week. It seemed so incredibly dismal, he wondered why on earth he'd stayed there.

"You're acting like a big baby."

Marli's forthright words played over and over in his mind, in sharp contrast to the pity he'd gotten from others and how they'd danced around any mention of the subject. He had to admire the way she just put things out there.

Including her feelings for him. He sat on his cheap couch, rubbing his face. He didn't deserve her love. He was starting to realize Lisa and Travis' affair hadn't been the sole cause of the disintegration of his. He had some responsibility, too. He'd known that all along, but just hadn't wanted to admit it.

He apparently wasn't very good at relationships, and Marli deserved better, with her sweetness and caring. But damn it, it had been so hard to leave her. It was wrong of him to want anything more with her. Happiness like she deserved was so far out of his reach he shouldn't even be thinking about it. But he wanted it. He wanted her. He wanted to be worthy of her, to be the man she saw him to be.

He cracked another beer. Then he stared at the bottle in his hand. He was headed back into some very bad habits.

Beer wasn't going to save him from his thoughts.

He had another whole week before he went back to work. His gut cramped at the thought of returning, of how his co-workers would look at him, and treat him.

Who the hell cared what they thought?

Marli wouldn't.

He finished the beer, then dropped the empty onto the carpeted floor. *Fuck.*

He stared up at the ceiling.

"Who's going to make the first move?"

He heard her voice again. It was so real, it was like she was in the room with him. He was going insane.

He sat up, shook his head. This had to stop. Now.

He knew what he had to do.

If it felt like years since he'd been to his apartment, it seemed like eons since he'd been to the home he'd shared with Lisa. She was still living there, she and the baby. He hadn't wanted the house, hadn't wanted anything, just wanted out.

* * *

She opened the door and stood there wide-eyed, open-mouthed. "Trey!"

He forced a smile. "Hi. Can I come in?"

She let him in and he followed her into the living room. He looked around and saw new baby paraphernalia—a car seat sat on the floor near the door, blankets and small toys scattered around. He looked at Lisa, the question in his eyes.

"He's right over there," she said, nodding toward a little bassinette. "Sleeping."

Trey forced himself to go over and peek in. He was still so tiny, eyes scrunched closed, little fists curled up. He gazed down at the baby, his nephew, Lisa's son, and tried to sort out all the emotions tangled inside him. And he knew. Knew this small life didn't deserve to be screwed up.

"He's a handsome little dude," he said finally, smiling faintly at Lisa. "Are you both okay?"

She nodded. She looked tired, wearing loose clothes over a body that was different than he remembered, and sadness shifted inside him.

"If you need anything—you and Aidan—you can call me. I know Travis plans to be here for you, but if he's not, if you need anything…"

She nodded slowly. "Thank you."

"Can we talk?"

"Sure," she said. "Would you like something to drink? Coffee? Iced tea?"

"No, thanks."

She moved farther into the room and took a seat in one of the chairs. He sat on the couch.

"I…I'm not sure why I'm here, exactly." Trey leaned forward, elbows on knees, hands clasped. "I just know I have to get on with my life and we've never talked about what happened. I just wanted to tell you that I know I wasn't a very good husband and I'm sorry for not being there for you."

She was silent, fingers twirling a lock of her long, dark hair. "You weren't a bad husband, Trey. But you're right…you weren't there."

"I'm sorry." How to explain that? Yes, his career was important to him, but it never should have been more important than his wife. He had to face the fact he had used his career as an excuse to not be there, not wanting to deal with the fact he didn't feel the same about Lisa as he had when they'd got married. He didn't know what had happened. He loved her, but in an affectionate, friendly way.

"Chicken and egg thing," he said, getting a confused look from her. He explained. "I didn't want to be at home because I didn't want to face the fact our marriage was over, but maybe if I'd been home more, our marriage would've been better."

"I'm sorry, too, Trey." She spoke with choked emotion. "I shouldn't have done what I did. I was lonely, but that's no excuse. I know if there were problems in our marriage, I should've talked to you about it, not someone else. And especially not your brother."

"I felt betrayed," Trey said, with difficulty. "But it's also a form of betrayal when you withhold your feelings, withdraw, don't share your feelings, hopes, fears and I guess we're both guilty of that."

"That's true." She looked surprised. "Wow, Trey, I can't believe you just said that."

He couldn't believe it either. Marli—he'd betrayed her that way, too. His chest ached.

"I felt like you let me down," Lisa said. "You weren't there and didn't seem to care. It was just all so…exciting. Travis was interested in me. He was there; he listened to me. He made me feel special. Desirable." She wiped her eyes with her fingertips. "You'll never know how guilty I feel about what I did. And not only have I messed up your life, my life and Travis's life, but I've messed up Aidan's life, too." Her voice broke. "He's so little and he doesn't deserve that. He hasn't done anything."

"We'll make sure his life isn't messed up," Trey said hoarsely. He cleared his throat. "I've been thinking about that. Sheldon Barnes' mother screwed him up because of all the nutso things she did to him. Look what happened to him." He shook his head.

"You're not comparing me to his mother!"

"God, no, that's not what I meant at all," he said hurriedly. "I'm just saying, what happens to a kid early in life affects him always. Yeah, our family is messed up right now, but we don't have to ruin Aidan's life. That's why I'm here, and I'll make sure Travis is here for you and for Aidan, or I'll kick his butt."

She laughed through her tears. "Okay."

He wasn't sure if he could forgive Lisa and Travis for what they'd done. Maybe some day. Forgiveness wasn't necessarily forgetting—that would certainly never happen—but maybe forgiveness was just committing to not dwell on what had happened. Maybe replacing painful, angry thoughts with positive thoughts about Aidan and the possibilities of his life would lead to forgiveness. Trey was determined he would never take out all his hurt and anger and feelings of betrayal on the little guy sleeping peacefully across the room.

"You're a good man, Trey," Lisa said.

Enough people kept telling him that, he might actually start to believe it. "Nah. I've made a lot of mistakes."

"Everyone makes mistakes. But we can learn from them."

He considered it. Sure, that was the cliché. But maybe he could learn to be a better husband, a better person, someone Marli could deserve.

"Trey, I don't know if you can ever forgive me, but we could try to start over."

He looked at Lisa and knew the answer to that deep inside him, and it had nothing to do with betrayal or forgiveness.

"It's too late, isn't it?" Her face shadowed with sorrow.

He nodded. "I'm sorry."

He had many other things he had to do. See his lawyer. His doctor. His supervisor. And most of all, his family. First, his brother.

* * *

Travis's mouth dropped when he opened the door to him. "Trey."

Trey wasn't sure how to handle this. "Hey."

"You're…back. We saw you on TV." He stood aside and motioned Trey into his apartment. "You finally got that bastard."

Trey nodded, ran a hand through his hair as he walked in. "Yeah. Finally."

"So…" Travis swallowed, eyes looking everywhere but at Trey.

"We need to talk."

Travis grimaced. "Yeah. I guess so." Trey took a chair, while Travis lowered himself to the couch. "I guess I should start. With an apology." He leaned forward, arms on his knees. "I don't know what else to say, except I'm really, really sorry, Trey."

There was a long silence, fraught with tension. "Why, Travis? Why'd you do that?"

"It's not a question of why I did it," Travis answered slowly. "It's more, why didn't I stop. I didn't set out to steal your wife. It just kind of happened. I'd drop by to see you and you were never there, and Lisa was. She was kind of lonely. We'd go out for coffee. We talked."

He hung his head. "I've always liked Lisa. Even before you two got married, but honest to God, I'd never have deliberately done anything. But she was there, and available and lonely, and it just happened.

"It's not an excuse," Travis added. "There is no excuse. I'm just telling you what happened. And I'm sorry. I should've done the right thing and just walked away. But I'm not strong and perfect like you."

Trey snorted, rolled his eyes at that.

"You have a nephew, Trey. You should see him."

"I already did." He paused. "You and Lisa?"

Travis shook his head. "We're not together. I'm going to be in Aidan's life, but things didn't work out with me and Lisa," he said gloomily. "She doesn't feel that way about me." He met Travis's eyes. "I think she's still in love with you, Trey."

Sadness pushed down on him. "We fell out of love a long time ago."

Silence weighed heavy for a moment.

"Mom and Dad are worried sick about you," Travis said. "So's Julie. You have to talk to them."

Hearing that reminded him of Marli and the things she'd said to him, and then he remembered… "Get up," he said.

"Huh?"

"Get up," he repeated in a hard voice, standing. His fists clenched at his side. Travis slowly stood. Trey moved around the coffee table and with a lightning-fast move, he drove his fist into his brother's gut.

Travis doubled over, moaning, then slumped into the chair.

"Get up!" Trey snarled again, nudging Travis's foot with his own.

"I deserve that," Travis croaked, huddled on the sofa, clutching his stomach.

Trey grabbed his brother's shirt and hauled him up. "Tell me you've always practiced safe sex," he snapped, his face right there in Travis's.

"What?" Travis struggled to get his wits back.

"Safe sex. Condoms. Tell me you always use them."

"Yeah. Yeah, of course I do."

"How'd Lisa get pregnant?"

"I swear, we used a condom," Travis said desperately. "It broke or something."

"And every other girl you've slept with?"

"Condoms. Always. I swear."

Trey threw him back down in the chair. "And did any of *those* break?"

"No!"

"You'd better be telling the truth."

Travis panted, staring at him.

Trey rubbed his forehead. Using his fists wasn't exactly improving his communication skills. What the hell was he thinking. "Sorry," he muttered.

"Feel better now?"

He glanced up and saw Travis's mouth twitch. A slow smile stretched his own lips. "Yeah, I do."

CHAPTER 24

Marli had spent the entire week picking up the pieces of her business and her life. She'd been on the phone constantly, sucking up to clients, rescheduling shoots, having business lunches. She'd been working late into the evenings, trying to get as much done as she could, so her clients didn't suffer for her disappearance.

Many had heard about what happened to her and were very understanding. A couple of others had taken their business elsewhere, and really, she couldn't blame them. It was business, after all, and if they needed photographs to advertise their products and there were publication deadlines and project timelines, they needed to get the job done somehow.

Shortly after Trey had left, her parents had shown up at her door from Newport, frantic with worry about what they'd been seeing on the news. They'd found her sitting on her kitchen floor, crying, which had alarmed them no end. She'd reassured them she was fine, perfectly safe, unhurt, but luckily they couldn't see her bruised and battered heart.

She also had dinner with her friends Jenn and Rachel, who'd left her a number of increasingly frantic voice mail messages. They'd been all over her with questions about what had happened and inquiries about Trey. She wasn't quite ready to talk about Trey yet, but she knew one day she would.

"It's so weird to not have Krista here," Rachel said sadly.

They all agreed. Marli shared her feelings of overwhelming guilt about how things had ended between her and Krista, and sharing it all again made it that much less painful. It was as if every time she talked about it expelled some of the guilt. Her friends reassured her Krista had loved her, and had known Marli loved her, too.

"You knew Krista," Jenn said. "Do you think right now, looking down on us, she's blaming you for what happened? Do you think she's up there saying, 'If only Marli had stopped me'?"

Marli shook her head. She could not imagine Krista saying or thinking that.

"She would *never* say that," Rachel said earnestly. "You *know* that. You were friends. You weren't responsible for her every move, every choice."

"I know," Marli said. "I know that now. I just wish things had ended with us not mad at each other."

"You two had a whole life of love and laughter," Jenn pointed out. "One fight doesn't negate all that."

It had helped to talk to her friends about it, just as it had helped to talk to Trey. She was so grateful he'd been there and been so understanding, letting her open up and share her feelings with him without judging her at all. If only he would do the same for himself.

Through all of it, her heart throbbed with a dull pain that turned sharp whenever she thought about Trey. Her heart ached for him, and what he'd been through, and it hurt for herself—for the thought that she'd never see him again.

* * *

Through the closed door, he could hear the thumping bass of loud music. Trey turned the knob and opened the door. The music got louder.

He walked into a huge open room, with high ceilings criss-crossed by a network of ductwork and pipes. The walls were all white save the long outside wall, which was natural creamy brick. Hardwood floors stretched to the far end of the room where a photo shoot was taking place.

Three women dressed in very little were arranged on and around a chaise longue upholstered in a plush leopard print fabric. The blonde with long, tousled curls wore a white lace bustier, thong panties and a garter belt, with white stockings on her long legs. The brunette, with similar long hair, was dressed in a black lace bra and tiny underwear that looked like shorts, and the redhead wore a bronze-colored satin camisole and thong. The scene glowed in the brilliant lights directed down on it, vivid and rich with color and texture.

A huge background hung from a large dowel suspended from the ceiling, rolling down behind them and across the floor. A woman dressed all in black made an adjustment to the bronze camisole, while another man and woman stood off to the side, watching.

Justin Timberlake was bringing sexy back to a throbbing beat booming from a killer stereo system sitting on a counter on one side of the room.

The scene was seductive with the three gorgeous models, but it was the photographer who drew his attention. She stood beside a camera mounted on a tripod with her back to him, long golden curls handing down almost to her waist. She was dancing, her hips moving temptingly in time to the music, watching and waiting as the woman in black made her adjustments, then scooted off the scene in her stocking feet. As he moved farther into the room, watching with fascination, the models all looked at him, and Marli turned to see what had distracted them.

Her lush mouth parted into a surprised O and she stilled, staring at him.

"Trey."

He smiled at her. Man, she was gorgeous. Her skinny jeans hugged those long, long legs and the thin T-shirt she wore over them outlined her curvy body. His heart was about to pound right out of his chest at the sight of her.

"Sorry. I'm interrupting."

She nodded, her green eyes huge. "Um…yeah." She glanced back at the models. "I need to finish this."

"Is it okay if I wait?"

"Sure. We're almost done." She licked her lips, which made him want to lick them, too, and turned back to the group posed before her. "Sorry, ladies," she said cheerfully. "Let's finish this up."

She moved back behind her camera and started shooting, firing off shots rapidly, while encouraging the models in their poses. The music changed to the Black Eyed Peas singing "Pump It", and Marli's body continued to move to the music as she worked. When she finally called a halt, the models stood up, stretched, and wandered off the set. He couldn't help but watch them with appreciation as they all went into a corner blocked off by screens.

He turned his attention back to Marli, who was grinning at him.

"Put your eyes back in your head," she told him, green eyes sparkling with humor.

"Hey," he said, "it's just nice scenery."

She nodded knowingly. "Very nice. Coquette Lingerie. I do all their photography."

The woman in black had been packing up some bags, chatting with the other couple, and now slung them over her shoulder. "I'm outta here, Marli," she announced, eyeing Trey. She smiled. "Nice working with you, as always. I guess I'll see you next week on that shoot for West Coast Mall."

"Yeah, you betcha. Thanks, Whitney."

"Thanks, Marli," called the other woman, picking up a purse and briefcase off the counter. "When will you e-mail me the link to the shots?"

"Tomorrow," Marli replied. "Then we'll talk."

The man and woman also left.

Trey looked around her studio. "This is impressive."

"Thanks." She went over to the big window on the outside wall and raised the thick black blind covering it. The room became lighter, but it had been raining all day, so the light remained weak and grey. She walked over to the camera and removed the memory card, took it over to a Mac computer on a desk.

"Just let me get these started downloading," she murmured, eyes on the monitor, one hand clicking the mouse. Then she straightened and went back to the camera. He watched as she deftly removed the camera from the tripod, twisted the battery compartment and removed the battery, then connected it to a recharger on the counter. She tucked the camera away in a camera bag.

Trey wandered over to look at framed photographs of her work on one wall. One by one, the models came out from behind the screen, now dressed in T-shirts and jeans or baggy cargo pants, looking decidedly less glamorous.

"'Bye, Marli," they all called, waving perfectly manicured hands as they left the studio.

And then they were alone. Trey swallowed nervously.

Marli unplugged lights, took down umbrellas and lowered the lights on their stands.

"So, how are you?" she asked. She removed a reflector from the light and put on some kind of cap.

"I'm good. Ah…you have a lot of equipment here."

She smiled. "Yes."

She continued her work, removing lights from the stands and putting them away in cases while he debated what to say.

"Not to sound rude, but what are you doing here?" she finally asked, folding up a light stand.

"I wanted to tell you what was happening with Sheldon Barnes."

"Oh. Okay."

"He's back in San Diego now, on suicide watch. He confessed everything, in fact, he confessed to even more murders than we knew about. He apparently went on for hours, confessing to killing about fifty women. The detective who interrogated him said he was a pretty smooth talker."

"He is," Marli confirmed, her voice sad.

"They said they could see how he used his charm to lure women to trust him. When they told him we were interested in him for five murders, he laughed and told them it was more like fifty."

Marli made a shocked noise, standing there with an umbrella in her hand.

Trey shook his head. "Don't necessarily believe that," he said dryly. "I'd never believe anything a sexual criminal tells me without hard evidence or witnesses. He'll deny, exaggerate, manipulate…basically lie through his teeth." Trey shook his head. "But he'd moved around so much, working on ranches, other odd jobs, he could easily have killed women in a lot of places and then just left town. They're reopening cases in Texas and New Mexico."

"Sounds like he loves the attention," Marli observed.

"Yeah, no kidding. Narcissistic personality. Exaggerating his exploits to impress people, grandiose fantasies. But eventually he stopped talking and asked for an attorney. Claimed to be totally innocent. Said he'd just been joking. All those women, he said he was just in the wrong place at the wrong time, just an unhappy coincidence."

"Bullshit."

He smiled.

"Trey, what makes someone do things like that?"

"Oh, lots of things." He ran a hand through his hair.

"Is he insane? Would they let him off because of that?"

Trey shook his head. "No. His behavior was too violent, although he definitely seems as though he has that sociopathic personality." He paused. "He had problems dealing with anger and, frustration. His upbringing had a lot to do with it. His relationship with his mother. All along, I believed he was getting his gratification from the thrill of controlling a woman…the power he had over her as he raped her. The power his mother had over him."

"Did she… Was he abused?"

"Emotionally abused, for sure. Some physical abuse. Not sure about sexual." He shrugged. "He was so angry at his mother, that's why his victims were always blonde women. That's why the murders were so brutally aggressive."

"Why did he stalk me, though?" she asked. "I was thinking about it, and it wasn't like the other murders. You said he'd always just leave after, go somewhere else."

"You laughed at him," he reminded her. "I recall that his mother laughed at him for wanting to be a cowboy, too. *And* you rejected him. It set him off and made him act outside his usual pattern."

She nodded slowly.

"You know, we all have the ability to distort reality in our minds, to protect ourselves, make us feel okay about ourselves. A psychopath already lies without remorse, but this just adds to that. He may well have convinced himself that he really wasn't doing anything wrong. He believed you'd really done something to him."

"Oh, God."

"Most of us can recognize we do that—that our perceptions aren't necessarily reality—but he wouldn't be motivated to do that, clearly, in trying to protect himself from being convicted and from a death penalty."

"You didn't come all the way here just to tell me that." She closed up a case of equipment with a snap.

His lips curved. "No. Maybe we could sit down somewhere and talk." He looked around.

Marli motioned to the leopard chaise, no longer lit by the powerful lights.

He went over and sat down, and she came and sat beside him, leaning against the curved back of it. A vision of her, clad in lingerie, lounging on the chair, flashed into his head and he almost groaned.

"Okay. So?" She looked at him encouragingly, her eyes a bit wary. She briefly bit her luscious bottom lip.

"So," he repeated, just drinking in the sight of her. "I don't know where to start. So maybe I'll just start here." He leaned forward, put one hand on her cheek and kissed her, closing the small space between their bodies on the chaise. She couldn't move back, and he took her mouth in a long, hot kiss.

She was warm and delicious, sweet and tempting, and God, he'd missed her. He lifted his head to look at her, brushing his thumb across her full bottom lip.

She looked sweetly dazed, green eyes dark with emotion. "Uh, wow."

He smiled faintly. Then they were at each other, mouths hungry, hands greedy, touching each other, pulling at clothes, sucking, licking, eating at each other.

He filled his hands with those breasts, high, full and soft, nipples hard against his palms, kissing her over and over. She moaned, writhed beneath him, and they shifted their bodies without a word, fitting themselves to each other, stretching out on the chaise. He pressed a thigh between her legs, feeling the soft heat there, and she arched into him, crying out softly. With one hand, he turned her face to him again, ate at her lips, licked his way into her mouth, played with her soft tongue.

He tried to get under her T-shirt, desperately needing to feel skin, but damn, it was long, and he had to pull and tug and lift her hips to get it up around her waist. Then yes, his hands were on skin, silky and warm, and he shoved the T-shirt up the rest of the way and tugged her bra down. He buried his face between her breasts, inhaled her, that spicy scent that was hers alone, then nipped at the full curve of one breast, licked over the hard nipple, took it in his mouth.

She grabbed his hair and pulled hard, but his hair was short and her hands slid out.

"God, Trey! Someone could come in."

"Who cares?" he asked, blind, mindless, focused on her beautiful tits. "Ah!" He sucked the other nipple and this time her hands pulled his head to her, holding him at her breast, her head falling back, eyes closed.

"I need you, Marli," he murmured. He sat up and pulled her with him. "Lift your arms, sweetheart." She obeyed him, and he whisked the T-shirt over her head, then quickly dispensed with the sheer bra. He knelt to take off her jeans, tossed her shoes aside, then unbuttoned his fly. He looked at her, hesitating.

It was a little arrogant to come walking in here and five minutes later be doing her on the couch. He didn't want to screw this up. She'd said she loved him, but suddenly he was unsure, knowing he'd hurt her before he'd left.

She lay on the leopard chaise, her hair a bright contrast to the gold and brown print, her pale gold body long, lean and gorgeous. Her eyes watched him as he paused, hands at his fly. Then she lifted her graceful arms to him, inviting him, welcoming him, and he dropped his pants and fell onto her.

He couldn't get close enough, couldn't get enough of her, because it would never be enough…never, never. He kissed her mouth, the side of her neck, her soft shoulders. His hands moved over her, exulting in the feel of her, parting her legs, dipping into her sweet wetness. The scent of her arousal rose around them, making him pant and driving him wild with need. He touched her clit, a hard, swollen bud and she jerked beneath him, raising herself against hand. He moved his fingers, rubbed her there, and she came apart in his arms, trembling and whimpering.

As her tremors slowed, he pushed her legs farther apart and slid into her, hot, soft and lush. With a long, shaky moan, she welcomed him in, opened for him, clasped him to her body with her strong, slim arms.

"You feel so incredible." He kissed her breast. "So fucking good. God, Marli."

He thrust harder, deeper, then her hands clawed at his back, tugged at his shirt. "A condom," she whispered raggedly. "Trey…"

"No." He buried his face into her neck. "No…it's okay…don't need it." And with a long, strangled groan, he poured himself into her, his heart thudding, ears roaring. He came and came and came, in long waves of hot pleasure that left him weak, so weak he wasn't sure he could draw in another breath.

He shifted off her just slightly, still holding her, still with his face buried in the soft, fragrant skin of her neck, gasping for breath. He'd had the impression of flying, high and limitless, floating back slowly down onto the chaise in Marli's studio.

"Oh, Trey," she said, sounding a bit disturbed.

"What?" He could not lift his head. He put out his tongue and licked her, making her shiver.

"You didn't use a condom." She gave his back a little swat.

"It's okay. You said you were on the pill."

"Yes, but—"

"Don't worry," he murmured, then kissed and licked her again, sucked on her flesh tenderly. His heart was beating closer to normal speed and he could now hear over the blood rushing through his head.

He felt her sigh.

"You'd better be here for a good reason," she said. "If you're here to break my heart again, I'm going to have to hurt you."

He lifted his head and looked her in the eye. "I love you, Marli."

She was silent. Then her lower lip trembled. "That's a pretty good reason," she said. "Oh, shit." She swiped at tears in her eyes. "I never used to cry," she told him fiercely. "I've cried more around you than I have since I was a baby."

"It's okay, sweetheart." He pulled her close. "You can cry in front of me any time you want."

"Good to know," she murmured. "Now tell me, what's going on? Am I having an affair with a married man?"

Direct, to the point... He loved that about her. "Are we having an affair?"

"I don't know. Are we? I don't have a hot clue what's going on here."

He laughed. "Okay, technically, yes, I'm still married, but the divorce is in the works. I saw my lawyer on Tuesday."

"Oh." He could feel her relief.

"And we're not having an affair."

"We're not?"

"No." He shook his head looked her steadily in the eye. "This is more than an affair."

"Oh."

"I also saw my doctor on Wednesday and got the test results Thursday. I'm clean, so nothing to worry about there."

Her smile was relieved. "So we were okay without a condom."

"Yeah. I went to see my parents, too. Let them know I'm okay. In fact, better than okay, thanks to you."

"You've been busy."

"And I went to see my boss at work."

"Oh."

"Yup. We had a good talk. Now I've got my shit together, I'm ready to go back to work. So I requested a transfer."

"Really? Hmmm." She put a finger to her lips, her eyes gleaming. "Let me guess. San Francisco, so you can work with Kent again? "

He laughed. "Wrong. I start in the LA office in two weeks. He agreed that starting fresh in a new office would be a good idea. I have to go back and clean up some stuff in San Diego, but I'll be moving here. Which leads to my next problem, which is, finding a place to live."

"Trey—"

"Wait." He held up a hand. "I'm not saying I want to move in with you. Not right away anyway. We really need time, I think. God, I'm not even divorced yet. I'm still no prize, that's for sure. I still have a lot of crap to deal with and I need to do that on my own."

"I can help you," she murmured.

"I know you can. I want you to. You've had a rough time lately, too. We can help each other. I need you, Marli. But I want to get established here, have a life, get to know you…take you on another date, maybe. And one day, when my divorce is final, we can see how things are going…"

"I can live with that."

"I'm here for the weekend, though," he said with a smile. "Maybe you can put me up just for a couple of days? I'd like to make love to you somewhere other than a hotel room."

"We just did," she pointed out.

He laughed. "Oh, yeah." Then he took a deep breath. "The other person I went to see this week was Lisa. And the baby."

"Oh, Trey." She sighed. "Was that hard?"

"Yeah, but not so much once I got there. We talked and got some stuff out in the open. But there still is one thing I need to tell you."

"What's that?"

"The fact that Lisa will still be in my life. I want to be up front with you because you're always up front with me. I told her if Travis ever reneges on his responsibilities to Aidan, if she ever needs anything, that she can call me. Because I don't want to see Aidan's whole life screwed up because the adults in his life can't get it together."

She gazed at him in silence.

"Is that a problem for you?" he asked, watching her, his insides knotting.

"You are so amazing," she said in a choked voice and kissed him adoringly. "God, I love you."

He kissed her back, relief and gratitude swelling in him. "Lisa and I were both responsible for our marriage falling apart," he said when they drew apart. "Once I admitted that, it was as if a huge load lifted off me. I still have to deal with their betrayal, but it somehow doesn't seem so bad."

"Yeah. I know what you mean. So, that's good."

"Lisa's going to have a rough time raising a kid on her own." He paused. "And," he continued, "the really good thing is that now I know I *have* feelings. I have feelings for you I've never felt before, so it's not all a tragedy."

She nodded.

"Being away from you put everything into perspective. What's important and what's not. Dwelling on the past and my own screw-ups is not important. I decided that's what forgiveness is—not dwelling on the negative. So I'm trying to stop beating myself up."

She eyed him solemnly. "You helped *me* to stop doing that. I knew if you could only do it for yourself, you'd be okay." She searched his face. "I thought…when you left…I thought maybe you were going back to try to work things out with Lisa."

"No." He pressed her head to his chest. "I haven't loved her for a long time, truth be told. There were problems in our marriage for quite a while. We didn't fight or anything. I just didn't feel the same about her. But instead of dealing with it, talking to her, I took the coward's way out and spent all my time at work."

"I would *never* let you get away with that."

"I know," he said fervently. "Please, Marli, don't ever let me get away with crap like that with you." He hugged her tightly. "But the person I need to be the most honest and open with about my own failings and feelings is *me*. I've been telling myself a lot of crap for the last six or seven months…or longer. Crap like talking about my feelings, or asking for help, is a sign of weakness. And look what happened." He sighed. "But you made me realize maybe I *do* deserve to be happy. Maybe I'm even good enough for you." He paused, his throat tight. "You saved my life, Marli."

She shook her head. "Uh-uh. Other way around, buddy, remember? You saved my life, like ten times." She teared up again. "God, what a suck I am." She brushed wetness away.

"Yes, you *did* save my life. I didn't know where I was going, what I was doing, when I met you. You made me laugh, you made me think about stuff I didn't want to think about. You made me want to be good enough for you."

"You are." She smiled at him. "You're the best man I've ever met."

"Nah." He denied it, even though he loved hearing it from her.

"Well, you're not perfect."

He laughed again. Trust her to keep his head from swelling too much. "I know. You showed me what a coward I am, and what real bravery looks like."

"Huh?" Her slender brows drew together.

"You put yourself out there every day," he said softly, touching her hair. "Telling me how you felt all the time. Telling me you loved me. *That* took real courage."

"Oh, Trey."

They shared a long, tender smile and he said, "There's more than one way to save a life."

KELLY JAMIESON

Kelly Jamieson is the author of several sexy romance novels. Her writing has been described as "blisteringly sexy" and "a spicy delicious read." She lives in Winnipeg, Canada, with her husband and two children. If she can stop herself from reading or writing, she loves to cook. She has shelves of cookbooks that she reads at length. She also enjoys gardening in the summer, and in the winter she likes to read gardening magazines and seed catalogues (there might be a theme here...) She also loves shopping, especially for clothes and shoes. But her family takes precedence over everything else (yes, even writing). She has two teenage children who are the best kids in the world, not that she's biased, and a wonderful husband who does loads of laundry while she plays on the computer, writing stories.

Kelly loves hearing from readers, so please visit her web site at www.kellyjamieson.com or contact her at info@kellyjamieson.com.

* * *

Don't miss *Worth Waiting For*
by Kelly Jamieson,
available at AmberHeat.com!

Ten years ago, Griff Campbell walked out of Ainslie Patterson's life without a word, breaking her young heart. Now, just when she thinks she's over him and has found love with someone else, he strolls back into her life, still as charming, playful and irresistible as ever.

Ainslie knows she's changed a lot in the last ten years, and she discovers so has Griff. So shouldn't the attraction between them have disappeared along with the people they used to be? But that pull between them is still there, unstoppable, unavoidable...unsettling. Why has Griff shown up after all these years? Just to lure her into his web of charm only to break her heart again? Or could they have something together now, something that was all worth waiting for?

16903877R00086

Made in the USA
Lexington, KY
19 August 2012